THE CLIQUE

SUMMER COLLECTION

CLAIRE

CLIQUE novels by Lisi Harrison:

THE CLIQUE
BEST FRIENDS FOR NEVER
REVENGE OF THE WANNABES
INVASION OF THE BOY SNATCHERS
THE PRETTY COMMITTEE STRIKES BACK
DIAL L FOR LOSER
IT'S NOT EASY BEING MEAN
SEALED WITH A DISS
BRATFEST AT TIFFANY'S

THE CLIQUE SUMMER COLLECTION:
MASSIE
DYLAN
ALICIA
KRISTEN
CLAIRE

THE CLIQUE

SUMMER COLLECTION

CLAIRE

A CLIQUE NOVEL BY LISI HARRISON

Poppy

Little, Brown and Company
Hachette Book Group USA
237 Park Avenue, New York, NY 10017
For more of your favorite series, go to www.pickapoppy.com

First Edition: August 2008

Cover design by Andrea C. Uva
Cover photos by Roger Moenks
Author photo by Gillian Crane

alloyentertainment

Produced by Alloy Entertainment
151 West 26th Street, New York, NY 10001

ISBN: 978-0-316-02750-2

10 9 8 7 6 5 4 3 2 1
CWO
Printed in the United States of America

For the Pretty Committee:
Thanks for a great summer! ☺

"Hey, sweetheaaaa't, can ya move a little faster? Mrs. Wilkes wants her plants watered by three and she's seven blocks away." Todd Lyons stretched out on the yellow terry cloth–covered chaise and folded his hands behind his head. His DON'T CHA WISH YOUR BOYFRIEND WAS HOT LIKE ME? T-shirt lay in a heap on the deck, and a swim coach's whistle necklace dangled above his gray, shark-covered swim trunks.

"I can't go to Mrs. Wilkes's." Claire skimmed the surface of the drowned bug–infested pool with a net. "I told you that last week." She wiped her beading forehead with the back of her hand, then dried it on her turquoise Gap drawstring shorts, her gray tank already too sweaty and no longer an option.

"I'll have to dock your pay." Todd unscrewed the top off a tube of zinc oxide and smeared the thick white cream all over his freckly cheeks. Combined with his shock of overgrown red hair and the yellow chaise, this made him look like a ten-year-old Ronald McDonald. But as a boss he was more like Jerk-in-the-Box.

"Whatevs." Claire skimmed the pool one last time, then dropped the long pole. It fell to the cement deck with a resounding clang. If she was going to be docked, why not

1

leave now? That way she could shower before her long-awaited reunion with her FBFFs (Florida BFFs) and style her hair with the cute flips on the bottom, the way Massie taught her.

Puuuuurp!

Todd blew his whistle. "Watch the attitude," he warned, his eyes closed and lifted to the sun. "And don't forget, Piper is booked for a walk and shampoo tomorrow morning at eight."

"I know." Claire pulled the bobby pin out of her hair and shook her long bangs loose. It was times like these when she wondered if working for her brother was worth it. But her goal was to earn enough money for a Massie-approved back-to-school wardrobe—or at least a cool pair of jeans—and so far, Todd was the only person in town willing to hire a twelve-year-old.

Maybe now that Sarah, Sari, and Mandy were finally back from sleepover camp, working for T-Odd Jobs, Inc. would stop sucking so much. Not that car washing, gardening, pool cleaning, dog walking, and bird sitting would suddenly become fun. Or that depending on her younger brother for a paycheck would become less pathetic. Or that doing *all* the work while he barked orders from the sidelines would become less humiliating. But with the girls around, life off the clock would be filled with side-splitting laughter, DIY crafts, and sugary snacks.

And it was about time.

Claire had waited all summer for summer to start. And with only four weeks left before her parents sold the house and moved everyone back to Westchester, she didn't want to waste another second.

Pedaling down Cherry Street on her old black and pink turbo Powerpuff Girls bike, Claire breathed in the citrus-scented air. She had missed the palm trees and orange trees over the last year. She had craved the thick, hot air that warmed her like one of Massie's old pashminas. And she loved making a wish every time a speedy little lizard zipped past her bare feet. As much as she'd grown to appreciate life in Westchester, Kissimmee was still home. And with the return of Sarah, Sari, and Mandy, it would finally start feeling like it.

Claire turned up the driveway of her soon to be ex–sky blue split-level ranch house, where three Razor scooters were lying on the grassy lawn beside the SOLD sign.

"Ehmagosh!" She jumped off her bike. It slammed to the ground, wheels still spinning.

"Ahhhhhh," shouted three girls from Claire's open bedroom window.

"Ahhhhh," Claire shouted back as she threw open the front door, bolted by her father, and took the peach-carpeted stairs two at a time. "You're early!" she called, silently telling herself not to worry about her toxic pits and limp hair. It wasn't the Pretty Committee on the other side of her Hello Kitty sticker–covered door. These were her down-to-earth, wear-the-same-pair-of-socks-three-days-in-a-row *sisters*. She'd never cared about her looks before. . . .

Still, a little effort might be nice.

After a quick extra-spitty lip lick (poor-girl's gloss) and a

3

speedy cheek pinch (PG's blush), Claire barged into her lemon yellow bedroom, her bare feet sinking into the white shag. To honor her friends' return, she'd salted the carpet with each of their glitter colors; blue for Mandy, pink for Sari, orange for Sarah, and green for herself. It looked like the entire Orange Bowl parade had melted on her floor.

"CLAIRE-BEAR!" The girls rushed toward her for a group hug, but Claire kept her arms pinned to her sides. It was either that or get nicknamed Bad Pitt by Massie, should word somehow get back to New York.

"Why so stiff?" Mandy pulled away, her thick dark eyebrows more noticeable than they had been a year ago.

"Is that a Westchester thing? Because I heard people are colder up there. No pun intended. Well, maybe a little pun intended. But when I say colder I mean emotionally. Not weatherwise. Even though weatherwise it's coooold." Sari fake-shivered, her thin upper lip disappearing against her slightly buckteeth.

"Maybe it's a New York tr-eeeend?" Sarah shimmied like a limbo dancer preparing to slip under the pole but looked more like someone who had taken muscle relaxants in a windstorm.

Claire smiled warmly. Mandy still refused to pluck her hairy eye visors! Sari still rambled when she was excited! And Sarah still had no rhythm! Like an old song that brings back memories of a long-forgotten crush, these quirky traits brought Claire back to that place she was just before she moved. A place where gloss was saved for class photos, blush was for Halloween, and body odor was perfectly natural.

"None of the above. I just have a little BO." Claire giggled.

"More like MO." Mandy lifted her long, thin arm and pointed at Claire's daisy fabric–covered twin headboard. The cheery white and green floral print had been poked with pushpins that held dozens of Pretty Committee photos. Shots of the girls lying on sleeping bags, piling in the back of the Range Rover, cheering at soccer games, carving the Chanel logo out of snow, dangling tuna sashimi from their mouths, latte-toasting at Sixbucks, flying on the Gelding Studios private jet to Hollywood, and several *Vogue* poses with the Massie-quin were all on display.

"What's MO?" Claire asked, half smiling, half fearing the answer.

"Moved On." Mandy pouted, her turned-out bottom lip looking extra pink against her ever-pale skin.

Claire's white blond eyelashes fluttered in confusion.

"Or Massie Obsession." Sari twirled her long blond hair, something she always did when goading someone.

"Or Meeee-*Owwww*," Claire purred like Catwoman, desperate to put an end to their teasing. Not because she couldn't take it, but because it forced her to consider the truth behind it, which she was nawt ready to do. Wasn't it possible to like both sets of friends equally?

"Or Making Out!" Sarah lifted the one photo that was facing backward, kissed it, and then buried it in her mess of short, dirty blond curls. But Claire still managed to catch a forbidden glimpse of her ex-crush Cam Fisher winking his green eye.

At the beginning of the summer, when she'd hung the picture, Claire had made a pact with herself not to look at it until Cam responded to one of the six I'm-sorry-for-spying-on-you-through-the-secret-camera-that-was-planted-in-your-sensitivity-training-class-and-I-will-never-do-anything-like-that-again-if-you-give-me-a-second-chance letters she'd sent him at summer camp. Now it was almost eight weeks later, and her mailbox was just as empty as her heart.

Seeing him now, even for a second, conjured the rich woodsy smell of his Drakkar Noir cologne and the heaviness that came with missing him. The sudden sensation was dizzying. Claire lowered herself onto the edge of her bed and sighed with the old squeaky springs, leaking joy like a punctured balloon.

Sarah sat gently beside her. "We're only kidding, Claire-Bear." Her sea foam green gauze pants scratched the side of Claire's thigh.

Sari sat too, covering her bony knees with her pink TJ Maxx sundress. "We just missed you. And these pictures prove you replaced us."

"I didn't *replace* you!" Claire stood. "You should see my computer. You guys are my screen saver *and* my wallpaper."

"Wow, *both*?" Mandy twirled her fingers in the air like a plate-spinner without plates. But more than the biting sarcasm, Claire noticed the black hair on her friend's arm. Maybe it wouldn't be as noticeable with a tan . . . or a sleeve. Anything other than a dishwater gray tank dress would have been a step in the right direction.

"Thank gosh *Dial L for Loser* was a flop or we would have lost you forever!" Sarah pulled the picture of Cam out of her hair and pinned it back to the headboard, facing forward this time.

"Opposite of true!" Claire blurted, stealing one of Alicia's lines.

"Whaddaya mean?" Sari play-smacked Claire's arm. "It tanked."

Claire burst out laughing. "I mean the part about *losing* me was opposite of true. I *know* the movie tanked."

They all cracked up a little more than necessary. And Claire couldn't help wondering if it was a way for them to release the stress that had been building up inside each one of them over the last year. Stress that came from constantly wondering if your best friend had found someone better.

But as they slapped the daisy-covered bed and wiped the giggle-tears from their eyes, the answer was obvious. They were getting their groove back. And things would stay that way, as long as Claire could show them that Massie and the Pretty Committee hadn't changed her a bit. Which wouldn't be *too* hard, right?

The giant thermometer screwed to the side of Mrs. VanDeusen's screen door read eighty-three degrees. Still, the old woman's petite white Chihuahua was shivering like he had just pioneered a night trek through the Himalayas.

Next door, a beige garage door groaned open, allowing a matching beige minivan to reverse down the smooth black driveway.

"I know how you feel, Piper." Claire knelt on the grassy front yard at the end of a Fisher Price–littered cul-de-sac. She lifted the frail puppy. His ribs were one missed meal away from total exposure. "I shook like that in Westchester. Mostly from the cold, but partly from the people." She giggled softly.

Piper blinked his bulging black eyes and licked Claire's cheek sympathetically.

"Awwww, thanks." She hugged the pup. "But you don't have to worry about me." Gently, she placed him on the warm pavement and wrapped the leopard-print leash around her wrist. "I've adapted."

Inside the minivan two girls, both younger than Claire, pointed at her and laughed. They were probably wondering if she was really talking to a dog.

8

With a light tug, Claire let Piper know it was time to move. Piper responded with a soft sneeze and a lively prance.

The thirty-minute walk paid thirteen dollars: seven to T-Odd Jobs, Inc., and the remaining six to Claire. Instead of feeling bitter about the inequitable split, she tried to put the time to good use by taking photos. The topic of the day was always the same: *Things I'll miss when I'm back in Westchester.* Whenever Piper stopped to sniff a flower or lick a flattened piece of street gum, Claire grabbed the Canon Elph out of her pear green cargo skirt and searched for things she'd stop seeing come September.

Two majestic palm trees standing side by side, like life-crushes.

Click.

A water rainbow in the Bennetts' sprinkler.

Click.

Her brown and pink polka-dot Keds.

Click.

Just then, Claire's red rhinestone–encrusted special-edition *Dial L for Loser* cell phone indicated that she had a text.

Kuh-laire!

It was Massie's personalized ringtone. Something she had recorded before they parted ways for the summer. Funny how what had sounded like an insult only a year ago suddenly felt endearing.

Her hands shaking like Piper's, Claire turned off the camera. After three days of no messages, an I-miss-u text seemed unlikely.

She led Piper to a crushed graham cracker on the sidewalk outside the Hobsons' house and sat on the curb. Once the dog was occupied, Claire inhaled deeply and opened the message.

Massie: Back 2 skl shopping list. For PC eyes only. Delete after purchasing.
ACCEPTABLE JEANS: J Brand, Joe's, Earnest Sewn, True Religion, Page, William Rast, AG, Rich & Skinny.
ACCEPTABLE TOPS: C&C, Vince, DVF, Splendid, L.A.M.B., Theory, Ralph (Alicia!), Ella Moss, Marc, and Juicy. Anything vintage as long as it doesn't smell like cat pee, moth balls, or old lady.
FOOTWEAR: Uggs (weekends only), Marc, Michael Kors, Calvin, anything sold on 7th floor of Barneys, no Keds!
MAKEUP: Must be bought at a DS (that's department store, not drugstore, Kuh-laire!). Anything by Be Pretty cosmetics is off-limits. They're dead 2 me.
ALSO OFF-LIMITS: All things shiny. Shiny is my back-to-school look. Anything purchased before June of this year (except vintage and jewelry.) Don't buy any silver charm bracelets from Tiffany. . . . You'll understand why when I see you. ☺
Text w/questions.
35 days till we're 2gether! YAYYYY! TTYL.

Piper yapped once at a circling bee before swatting at it with his front paw. He missed, then licked the ground where his cracker had been. Claire sighed. Why couldn't her life be that simple? Instead, she had wasted most of her summer working for Todd. And for *what*? A grand total of $167.70? *Gawsh!* The only thing she could afford on Massie's list was something vintage . . . from the Salvation Army. And *maybe* the cost of dry cleaning it.

More than anything, Claire wanted to text Kristen and ask—in total pinky-sworn confidence—how she, being financially challenged as well, could afford the things on the list? But she resisted. What if Kristen told? Reminding Massie that Claire couldn't keep up might jeopardize her place in the Pretty Committee. And who wanted to start eighth grade off like *that*? Especially when she was already getting the silent treatment from Cam.

Instead, Claire texted Massie back using the Visa philosophy of "buy now, pay later." Or in her case, "*lie* now, pay later."

Off to the mall ASAP! Wish U were here.

Once the message was sent, Claire bit her longest nail, wondering just *how* much she'd have to pay.

Another text.

Amnesia much? I AM here! Let's do it!

Claire's heart tightened and curled into the fetal position. *Here?* Massie was *here*? How was that possible? She re-read the text, hoping to see a "JK ☺."

BTW call me Amandy. Everyone at camp did. It makes me sound 16, right?

Claire checked her screen. MANDY! It said MANDY! She'd accidentally sent her text to Mandy. Not Massie! She was free to wear machine washables and slip-ons for thirty-five more days.

Claire wiggled her toes happily inside her Keds and bent down to hug Piper. He coughed once, then puked graham cracker.

Mandy: Right?
Claire: Right! Luv the new name!

With renewed purpose, Claire tugged Piper's leash. One more lap around the block and she'd be six dollars richer. It wouldn't get her any closer to a Massie-approved wardrobe, but it *would* get her a medium bag of sours at the Candy Baron and a large raspberry Slushee.

Mandy: At camp we were SAS: Sarah+Amandy+Sari.
Now that UR back we can B SACS!
Claire: Finally a SACS i can afford to be in ☺
Mandy: LOL!

A geyser of 100 percent pure *yay*-water shot through Claire's body. She was part of her Florida group again. The awkward readjustment period had officially ended.

Mandy: Wait until Miss Kiss! We're going 2 dominate!!!

Claire was about to text back to remind her friend that they were too young to enter the local pageant. But then she remembered—they were *twelve*. They qualified! All the years they'd spent honing their special talents, de-frizzing each other's hair, practicing their puckers . . . and now it was here. They were finally eligible to compete in the local teen Miss Kissimmee beauty pageant and—

Ugh.

Suddenly, a tangle of uneasy feelings corked up Claire's *yay*-water geyser. She rubbed her belly while Piper lifted his shaky hind leg and peed on the tire of a royal blue Honda Accord. *Why the sudden stomach pit?* The Miss Kissimmee pageant was something they'd dreamed of for as long as she could remember—hair, makeup, clothes, press, prizes, competition . . .

Double ugh! Competition. That was it! There were endless stories of lifetime BFFs who broke up over Miss Kiss. Just last summer it had happened to identical twins. The Bernard sisters, who to this day denied being related. And after the year she'd just spent in Westchester, the last thing Claire wanted was to compete with her best friends.

Mandy: I'll call SS and we'll go shop 4 R qualifying gowns.

Claire: I'll be UR manager.

Mandy: ?????

Claire: I'm moving. If I won, which I so wouldn't, it's not like i'd be able to go to the food court openings or football parades anyway.

Mandy: What about the $$$$.

Claire: ? $.

Mandy: $1000 4 1st prize!

Claire stopped so suddenly Piper practically choked. She couldn't take her eyes off Amandy's text. One thousand dollars! Piper started licking her big toe, and Claire started eating her words. "What's a little healthy competition between friends?"

After promising to meet Amandy's mother at the Nike outlet in thirty minutes, SACS hurried into Dress Barn. A cold blast of air-conditioning stung their bare arms and promised to keep them alert while they navigated rows of bright patterns and durable knits. And the instrumental version of "4 Minutes" by Madonna, Justin Timberlake, and Timbaland guaranteed they'd have a good time doing it.

"Gather." Amandy stopped below a mannequin wearing a brown and green polka-dot dress and gold sandals. She scanned the store like she was searching for eavesdroppers, and smiled when she realized they were the only pageant-worthy customers. "I've done some research on Miss Kiss, and in the spirit of sisterly love, I'm going to share."

"Ready!" Sarah pulled a Bic pen out of her short curly blond hair and held it above her palm. Sari gave her a thumbs-up as if to say, *Good job for staying on top of the whole note-taking thing.*

The S's were wearing slightly different shades of pink tank tops, and their cutoff jean shorts were covered in glitter hearts made up of their signature colors: pink for Sari and orange for Sarah. A camp art project, no doubt. Amandy, however, had chosen to memorialize her summer with a wristful of colorful boondoggle and macramé bracelets. They added

15

a cool, rugged touch to her adorable periwinkle blue J.Crew cotton sundress.

Claire felt a flash of jealousy. *Why had she ever let Massie convince her that homemade jewelry was unattractive?* Braided leather would have looked so edgy with her mint green cargo mini and yellow cap-sleeve Ella Moss tee (a hand-me-down from Dylan).

"Get this," Amandy whispered, a thin blue vein bulging along her temple. "In the past five years, the girls who qualified for the pageant were all wearing fruit-colored dresses. No earth tones. No solid white. No black." She snickered, then rolled her blue eyes. "As if we would ever."

Sari leaned over Sarah's hand to make sure she was getting all of this.

"What about patterns?" Sarah lifted her pen.

"No one ever got rejected for wearing florals, put it that way." Amandy smoothed her thick dark brows as if all this free advice was taking its toll.

"And length? Because it's super important to get the right length, because I mean, it could be at the ankle or at the knee or above the knee, or I mean even midcalf. I just want to make sure, you know?" Sari asked while stuffing a handful of candy corn in her mouth. Instinctively, she held out the Ziploc for the others, and everyone helped themselves. A delicious rush of sugar went straight to Claire's jaw. First chewy, then grainy, then liquidy sweet. The overall sensation was kind and loving—a welcome change from the sharp, spiteful corners of the low-fat Baked Lays she'd been snacking on all summer.

"Nothing above midthigh. It's the Miss Kiss, not the Miss Look-at-This."

S and S cracked up. Claire tried. But after a year of Massie's clever comebacks it was impossible to settle for anything short of brilliant.

"Can you believe we're actually *here*?" Sarah looked around Dress Barn like she was Dorothy landing in Oz.

Um, no! Claire could practically hear Massie say. "It's so exciting," she managed, finally locating her own voice. "We've waited all these years and—"

"Save it for the judges." Amandy elbowed Claire playfully. "Let's shop!"

Sari casually stuffed her empty Ziploc in the mannequin's green and brown polka-dot pocket.

"Um, security!" Sarah fake-called.

"You saw *that*?" Sari cracked up.

"Security!" Claire and Amandy joined in until they were slapping each other's shoulders in hysterics, barely remembering what had been so funny in the first place. Once they finally stopped, Clare's abs ached with soreness and her heart buzzed with joy.

"Meet at the dressing rooms in ten?" Amandy ask-insisted, subtly reminding them why they were there.

Seconds later the girls split like overprocessed hairs, each claiming a different part of the Barn. Claire wandered into the greens and yellows, where a cheerful shift dress caught her eye. It was the perfect length, and its flowers were definitely fruit colored—banana and kiwi, or was it more of a lime? She pinched the hem area and gave it a little rub between her index finger and thumb. The fabric was coarse and porous. Something Piper would definitely be able to hear with her sensitive dog ears. Claire released it quickly and peered across the store to see if her friends were having similar reactions to the rash-inducing material. But SAS were piling outfits onto their bent arms like they had won an hour of free shopping at Bloomingdale's.

Claire tried to imagine the Pretty Committee in this store, where the average dress cost thirty dollars and size twenty-fours were welcome. But she couldn't. In her mind the PC and the Dress Barn refused to fuse, like oil and water. Curdled milk and coffee. Angie and Jen. She could, however, imagine Massie making some kind of joke about how the store must be called the Dress Barn because the clothes were for animals. And for a second she actually missed the alpha. A second later, she missed her old sweet self.

Suddenly, Claire started to sweat. Her stomach cramped and her heart accelerated. The vibrant colors of the Dress Barn surrounded her, yet she was unable to move. Old photos told her that bright greens, yellows, pinks, corals, and turquoises flattered her—even more so now that she had a tan. And statistics proved that the judges liked these colors. But something was stopping her from bending her own arm and piling on the options.

That something was Massie.

Thanks to *her*, Claire knew too much about good quality and bad taste. After spending the last year surrounded by delicate hand-washables and dry-clean-only designerwear, she had developed an appreciation for good quality. She just hadn't realized it until now. And without the money to do anything about it, that knowledge made her feel like she was in a polyester-covered prison cell.

Ducking for cover behind a circular rack of knit cardigans in a rainbow of colors, Claire fired off a quick text.

Claire: Going 2 a VIP ball. Dress must be flirty, fun, & flattering. No black. Any suggestions?

A response arrived within seconds.

Massie: The 3Fs? No prob. Miu Miu has an ivory dress w/floral-shaped sequin embellishments. It's feminine without being overly girly and can be dressed up or down to suit the mood. Great with a Stella McCartney bag and Jimmy Choo shoes, 100% silk, inserts: 75% acetate, 25% viscose. Dry clean only. Note: Italian sizing.
Claire: ☺ thx.

Instantly, Claire began flipping over the dress labels in search of silk. But rayon and polyester blends were all she could find. Giving up, she hurried toward the ivory section, where, as luck would have it, a mannequin was wearing a cute A-line dress with tiny floral-shaped sequins. The flowers were brown (earth tone ☹) and the dress was cream-colored (white ☹), but it hit at the knee (Miss Kiss, not Miss Look-at-This ☺), was close to Massie's Miu Miu (☺), and cost $32.95. (☺ ☺ ☺ ☺ ☺)

Claire hurried to the closest mirror and slipped the dress on over her clothes. Once the bulk of her cargo skirt and Ella Moss shirt were gone it would fit perfectly. All she needed was a pair of brown slides and—

"Find something?" Amandy appeared behind her, squinting at the hanging white dresses as if their brightness was hurting her eyes. A cherry-red, poppy-covered empire-cut dress swung from her finger on a clear plastic hanger.

"Yup." Claire put her hands on her hips and turned to face her friend.

"Looks like lumpy oatmeal," Amandy sneered.

"You like?" Sarah danced over barefoot. Her knees were semi-bent and her palms were facing out, shifting back and forth like windshield wipers. She seemed to be moving to the upbeat tempo of "4 Minutes," even though that song had ended a while ago and now a whiny ballad was playing instead. She was wearing a blue, orange, and yellow kerchief dress. It was bohemian chic, and flattering in the relaxed sort of way that her dance was not.

"Cute." Claire smiled and meant it. "Gold sandals would be so ah-dorable with that."

"Really?" Sarah tugged one of her curls. "I was thinking my blue jellies. They have a perfect little kitten heel!"

Claire literally bit her tongue to keep from commenting. *Had her friends always had such bad taste? Should she intervene? Was this how Massie felt around her?*

"I thought we were meeting at the change rooms," Sari whined. "I was standing back there forever and ever and ever and then I finally gave up and came looking for you out here, and thank goodness I did, because here you are!" Then she held a pale pink, pale yellow, and pale green paisley dress up to her long torso. She adjusted her long blond hair so that it cascaded over her shoulders, then licked her thin lips and puckered. "Mwah!"

"Ew!" Claire blurted. She was about to add that it looked like a box of Good & Plenty had melted all over the dress. But she held back when she saw Sari's pointy chin start to tremble.

"I knew it. You *have* changed!" Amandy cried.

Sarah raised her black brows and mouthed, "Ouch!" But she didn't say a word in Claire's defense.

"We used to pick out the same clothes all the time, like when we both reached for those canary yellow overall shorts, or the hot pink Keds slip-ons, or that awesome hat with the plastic sunflowers on it, just like the ones that go on bikes," Sari pouted. "Remember?"

"I do," Claire said, solemnly at first. And then quickly managed an enthusiastic smile. "I mean, I still *do* have the same taste as you." She reached for Sari's dress and gripped the bristly material. It felt like the surface of the rocks they used to tan on in the Kissimmee state park, back before Amandy had done her science project on melanomas.

"*EW* means I love it. It stands for . . ." Claire paused for a moment. Extra wacky? Extremely woeful? Ever-so-wrong? ". . . *Extremely Wearable*."

"It does?" Sari's chin stopped quivering and her expression softened.

"Of course. What did you *think* it meant?" Claire heard her own voice but hardly recognized it. Was she acting kind or cruel? Sensitive or manipulative? Compassionate or competitive? Or had she evolved into some deviant species that was an enigmatic combination of them all? Wait until Layne heard about this. She'd be begging to draw her blood and analyze her hair and—

"It sounded to me like you didn't like it, like because *ew* usually means 'ew' as in 'gross,' or 'disgusting,' or 'that's so awful' or whatever, so I thought maybe you didn't like it, which was kind of depressing, because usually we like the same things." Sari picked at the pink heart on the left leg of her shorts.

"I *love* it." Claire used every ounce of her acting training to sound convincing.

"Prove it." Amandy pulled the elastic out of her ponytail. Her dark brown hair, which was always semi-damp, fell to her shoulders.

"How can I *prove* it?" Claire's heart beat harder. *Could Piper hear it? Could Bean?*

"*You* buy the dress." Amandy smirked.

"But Sari found it first. That would be unfair," Claire tried. "To *her*."

"Hi. I'm Louise. Everything okay over here?" asked a short, round, brown-haired woman wearing a maroon knit cardigan over black wide-leg trousers. Both items gave off a polyester sheen under the track lights. She clasped her plump hands and grinned, trying to look patient while she waited for an answer.

"We're fine, thank you," Claire finally offered.

"Will you be purchasing these items?" Louise gestured toward the register in the center of the store.

"Well?" Amandy said.

"I can't take your dress," Claire insisted to Sari.

"Sure you can." Sari handed it to her. "Yours is super cute. It reminds me of a Miu Miu dress I saw on Bluefly."

"But it's not the right color. I wasn't getting it for the pageant." Claire bit her thumbnail. An old Kelly Clarkson song came on over the loudspeaker.

"I can make it work." Sari piled her hair on top of her head and winked. "It's EW."

"Is mine EW?" Amandy asked.

"Super EW!" Sarah said.

"Does this mean you will *not* be purchasing the dresses?" asked the saleswoman.

Sari tossed the Good & Plenty dress over Claire's shoulder and grabbed a fresh Miu Miu knockoff from the rack. "No." She beamed. "It means we *will*."

"Lucky for you all of the dresses you chose today are twenty-five percent off."

Claire smile-sighed.

"Except yours." Louise pointed at Claire. "That's still fifty-nine ninety-five. You have wonderful taste. It's the most expensive piece in the Barn fall collection."

"Totally worth it." Claire beamed, knowing her friendship with SAS was more valuable than money. All she'd have to do was walk Piper ten more times and she'd have her savings back.

Her pride, however, would be gone for good.

"Pull the rake closer," Claire instructed Todd. "And wipe the sweat off your forehead—it's giving me glare."

Todd lifted the bottom of his red T-Odd Jobs tee and wiped his face. "Better?"

Claire lifted her camera. She took five action shots of her brother in their front yard as he fake-raked a pile of palm fronds off their otherwise spotless lawn.

This photo would represent "gardening" in the T-Odd Jobs free downloadable wallpaper series—a little something he wanted to leave for his customers after he moved. It was his way of "giving back" and showing them how much he valued their business. And it was Claire's way of recouping some of the money she'd lost on the Good & Plenty dress.

"We got it," Claire announced, consulting her shot list. "Moving on."

- Car Washing/Ride Pimping
- Pool De-Bugging
- Garage Organizing & Uncool Toy Removal
- Wardrobe Consulting
- Face Painting
- Doggy Day Care

- Gardening & Flower Arranging
- Reading to Small Children

"Let's set up for reading."

Todd dragged his navy blue Fatboy beanbag under the small circle of shade provided by their leafy red maple. He surrounded it with X-Men action figures and a stack of Dr. Seuss books. Once in position—legs crossed and leaning toward Wolverine, Magneto, Storm, Cyclops, Sabretooth, and Toad—he slid on their father's old wire bifocals. "Ready!"

Claire sighed and propped her camera. The light was poor, but she didn't have time to make adjustments. She had walking practice with SAS in twenty-five minutes—twenty of which would be spent getting up the courage to leave the house in her registration dress—so she clicked away while Todd shifted and read aloud from *One Fish Two Fish*.

"Is this the Lyons *estate*?" a man called from a brown delivery truck.

Todd burst out laughing. So did the deliveryman when he looked at the quaint sky blue home sandwiched between two other quaint homes. But Claire failed to see the humor. Since when did UPS guys make jokes about the size of people's houses? Okay, maybe in Westchester, but *here*?

"Are you Kuh-laire Lyons?" He stepped out of the truck, clipboard in hand. The gorilla-ish amounts of white blond hair on his arms matched what was left on the sides of his sunburned head.

"Yeah." Claire hurried toward him, her bare feet crunching down on the prickly piles of Todd's raked fronds.

He yanked his metal handcart from the truck, then wrestled to pull a five-foot-tall wardrobe box from the back. "Where do you want it?"

"Um, inside, I guess." Claire hurried to open the front door, standing back to allow the deliveryman to wheel the box into the small foyer.

"Sign." He thrust a clipboard into her hands and slid the cart out from under the box. "I guess one of your *estate* butlers will take it from here." He snickered.

"Very funny," Claire said with a sarcastic smirk, closing the door behind him.

"Open it!" Todd urged as he rooted through the mess of papers on the white vestibule table. He found their mother's silver-plated Bank of America letter opener and handed it to his sister.

Claire stepped up on the hallway bench to reach the top of the box and stabbed at the packing tape along the seams. A gust of Chanel No. 19 wafted out, like she had just released Massie Block from a genie bottle. Claire opened the front cardboard flaps and saw a note pinned to a white, wrinkle-free wardrobe bag. She lifted the purple card and read:

Are we hair dryers?

Claire said, "No," as she flipped the card over.

Then there's no need for outlets!

"How did she know I was at an *outlet*?" Claire wondered aloud.

"What is it?" Todd looked up at his sister as if admiring the Statue of Liberty.

Claire unzipped the bag and anxiously dug her hand inside. The textures were unmistakable. Denim, silk, beading, ruching, leather, suede, buttery-soft cotton (Splendid!). "It's a gift from my fashion gawdmother!"

"For what? Staying away all summer?" Todd snickered at his not-so-funny jab.

"She must have sent these for me to wear to the *ball*!" Claire thank-hugged the box as if it were Massie.

"What ball?" Todd ducked under Claire's arm and peered inside the box. "Whoa!"

"Long story." Claire nudged him back. She was so excited she didn't know what to do first. The clothes *felt* great. She couldn't wait to play her Miley Cyrus CD and try them on. But more than that, she was excited times ten by the gesture. Massie must have truly considered her a BFF if she had gone to the trouble of sending such an extravagant gift. Everything her parents had told her about Massie was right: *"She only acts mean because she's insecure. And lashing out makes her feel safe. On the inside she is a caring, thoughtful person who will show kindness and let down her guard once she knows she can trust you with her feelings."*

Well, it was beyond clear from the size and thoughtfulness of the gift that that time had finally come. Not only would Claire dominate the style rounds of Miss Kiss, but she could return to Westchester and Octavian Country Day School knowing for certain that she was 150 percent *in*.

"How jealous will Sarah, Sari, and Mandy be when they see this?" Todd asked, licking his devil-red lips in pleasure.

Claire's insides dipped like she was careening down Magic Mountain. "Ugh, I forgot about *that*." She hopped down off the bench to the floor. Had the ceramic tiles been that chilly a few minutes ago?

"Why so sad?" Todd put his clammy palm on Claire's tanned shoulder.

"Since when do *you* care?" Claire wiggled out from under his grip.

"A depressed employee is bad for business."

At that moment Claire would have traded every dime she'd ever made for a neutral friend to talk to. Someone who didn't care what she wore, whom she hung out with, or where she shopped. But Layne was at a weeklong science clinic with some friends from her summer school class. And Claire was dead to Cam.

Unfortunately, it looked like Todd would have to do.

"Long story short," she began, "I'm auditioning for Miss Kiss on Saturday, and Massie sent me a box of ah-mazing clothes to wear. But if I wear them, Sarah, Sari, and Mandy-whonowgoesbyAmandy will say I've become 'all Westchester' and that I think I'm too cool for Dress Barn, so I have to wear . . ." She lifted her finger, letting Todd know she'd be back in a second. After a quick dash to her bedroom closet, Claire returned with the EW dress. *"This."*

"It looks like someone barfed jellybeans on it," Todd giggled.

"I *know*." Claire stomped her bare foot in frustration.

"So why not let them pick dresses from the Massie box too?" Todd suggested, swiping his red hair off his still-shiny forehead.

Claire paused. For the first time in ten years, her brother had said something constructive. But after a second of contemplation, she shook her head.

"I can't. They'll think I don't like the dresses they bought and that I'm—"

"What's this?" Judi Lyons asked as she bounced downstairs in her lemon yellow tennis dress. She hadn't played in years, but she thought the pleated mini was still flattering and hated to see it go to waste. The sun had turned her shoulder-length brown hair dark blond ("free of charge!"), and she had decided to "go with it" until she returned to Westchester.

"Clothes." Claire beamed with pride. "From Massie."

Judi smacked her own forehead. "That reminds me, Kendra called."

"*Why?*" Claire asked, hoping the Blocks hadn't suddenly decided to rent their guesthouse to another family.

"The message said something about hoping I don't mind the intrusion. She must have been talking about this box."

"Tell her we don't mind!" Claire urged.

"I will." Judi kissed the top of Claire's head—a kiss that said, *I am happy you're happy.* She palmed the white wicker vestibule table. "Shoot. My keys are upstairs. Be right back, then we can head out."

"Where are you guys going?" Todd screeched. "We're in the middle of shooting!"

"I told you I had walking practice at Dipper Dan's." Claire threw the Good & Plenty dress over her shoulder as if it was a dirty towel. "And I already got the reading shot."

Todd spread his arms out. "How'd I look?"

"Great," Claire sighed.

"Jealous?" Todd asked, smiling at the dress.

"It's not funny! What am I gonna do?"

Todd tapped his freckly chin and looked up at the ceiling fan. "Hey! Remember that time Massie 'accidentally' spilled a latte on Kristen's church dress so she wouldn't have to wear it to the Easter dance?"

Claire giggled at the memory.

"Welllllllll?" Todd winked.

"How much?" Claire groaned.

"I want the T-Odd Jobs photos for free." He folded his arms across his red T-Odd Jobs shirt and made his hard-bargain face.

"Of course you do." Claire rolled her eyes, but she shook his hand. "Deal."

The coarse fabric of the dress rubbed the backs of Claire's legs raw on the fifteen-minute car ride to the local ice cream parlor.

"I'll be back in an hour," Judi called as her kids slipped out of the red Pontiac Torrent. "Stay together!"

"We will," Todd lied as he ducked down behind the car and ran across the strip mall parking lot toward the roof of the Publix grocery store. His T-Odd Jobs tee was swollen with five iced tea–filled balloons.

"Don't worry." Claire smile-waved at Amandy, who was just getting out of her father's silver Saturn convertible in front of Payless. She was wearing her poppy-covered empire dress. The vibrant color popped against her pale skin and electric blue eyes. With an eyebrow wax she might have been a nine. But her damp brown hair and unibrow lowered her score considerably. Not that Claire held it against her oldest friend. She was just grateful Massie wasn't there to witness the crime.

She and Amandy stepped onto the curb in front of Dipper Dan's and weaved through the crowd of people licking and sweating under the shade of the pink and white–striped awning. Just then, the jingle of the store's doorbells chimed. Sarah and Sari pushed through, each carrying two double-scoop cones of mint chip and cookie dough. They were wearing plastic lobster bibs around their necks, which obviously came from What's the Catch?, the seafood restaurant four doors down that Sari's father owned.

"It's packed in there, so we ordered for you." Sarah shoulder-brushed a blond curl away from her cheek as she handed Claire her cone.

"Do you have any extra bibs?" Amandy asked as she took her cone from Sari.

"Just one." Sarah pouted. "They're completely out. You can flip for it." She pointed at the nickel in her clear plastic change purse.

"That's okay," Claire blurted. "Mand—I mean *Ah*-mandy can have it," she said, still trying to warm to the annoying camp nickname. "The colors of my ice cream are the same colors as my dress. No one will notice if I spill."

Amandy speed-tied the bib around her neck, obviously trying to prove possession in case Claire changed her mind.

Without having to say it, SACS lick-walked toward the back of Publix. The huge grocery store had a wood loading dock for its delivery trucks, and after 3 p.m., when the deliveries stopped, it made a great runway. The girls had been using it (after all, it was Publix property!) for years.

"How EW are these dresses?" Sarah twirled in the middle of the parking lot, her blue, orange, and yellow kerchief dress lifting in the soft breeze. Eventually she lost her balance and slammed into a champagne-colored Cadillac sedan in the handicapped spot.

A group of high school boys *whoot-whooot*ed as they screeched past in a black Mustang, blaring "Sugar, We're Going Down" by Fall Out Boy.

SACS cracked up. The warm, humid air wrapped itself around their laughter like one big hug. And despite the suffocating heat, Claire's arms Brailled with goose bumps.

"I love my dress too. In fact, I love it so much I can't decide what I love most about it—the sequins, the Cookie Crisp color, or the way it draws attention to my shoulders and away from my arms. I just love, love, love, love, love it!" Sari parted her thin lips and poked her tongue into the green scoop of ice cream. "Sar, did you see those three guys ahead of us in line wearing the Dr. Sveningson Chiropractic baseball jerseys?"

"You mean the ones checking you out?"

"Yeah!" She squeal-grabbed Sarah's arm.

Claire tried not to hate Sari for switching dresses, but every time the wind blew the porous, candy-colored dress against her chafing skin it got harder. And when she caught a glimpse of her Pepto and lime–swirled reflection in the warped metal Publix delivery door, it became unbearable.

"And if anyone can pull off that wild pattern it's Lyons." Amandy patted Claire on the back like she was a real trouper.

"Thanks," Claire moaned, knowing she was.

They finally reached the dock in the loading area, which smelled like fish, raw meat, and cardboard. Still, the rancid combination brought comfort to Claire. She associated the smell with imaginary fashion shows, off-key Broadway musical renditions, and fake Miss Kiss contests. It was hard to believe they were there to practice for the real thing. And even harder to believe that after years of tearing out pictures of dream dresses for the pageant, Claire was wearing *this*!

She glanced up at the roof and saw the top of her brother's red hair. *Yes! He was there!* Todd, like a good sniper, was crouched down, waiting for the right moment. Claire sighed with relief, not the least bit concerned about the pain she might feel upon impact. Even if the balloon left a welt, the wound would heal—unlike the emotional scar she would have if forced to stand before a panel of judges in something that felt like burlap and looked like a preschooler's refrigerator art.

"Let's do it!" Amandy declared, lifting herself up onto the elevated wood platform.

Claire and the others followed. Once up, they stood tall and proud, like they'd finally earned the right to be there.

"Okay." Amandy wiped her hands on her bib. "We're gonna run through three walks." She lifted her thumb. "One: gliding over to the judge's table for sign-up." She lifted her index finger. "Two: gliding out of the room to the waiting area." She lifted her middle finger. "And three: gliding back in for the one-on-one interview."

Sarah and Sari lined up behind Amandy. Claire shuffled to the back. She casually lifted her eyes toward the roof to see if—

"Ahhhhh!" Sari screamed as a trickle of brown liquid spilled down the side of her dress. "I've been *shot*!" She rubbed the bright red circle on her arm where the balloon had hit, her eyes pooling with panic-tears. She looked down, as if expecting to see blood but finding something worse. "My dress!" The ivory was now stained the color of sewage.

"What *was* that?" Amandy shouted.

Smack!

"Ooof!" Amandy lurched as she took one in the back. "They got me!"

Smack!

A yellow balloon exploded at Sarah's feet. "You gotta love these jellies," she gloated. "They're totally waterproof."

Unfortunately, Claire's dress was still intact.

"Todd!" she blurted, waving her arms at the roof.

"Well, stop moving around so much!" Todd yelled back, his slightly raspy voice filling the empty spaces between the green-and-white eighteen-wheelers and the rusty metal trash bins.

SAS turned and glared at Claire.

Oops.

"You *knew* about this?" Sarah hissed just before she got nailed on the head. Her drenched blond curls dripped onto her kerchief dress and streak-stained the satin. "NO!"

"Sorry!" Todd called.

"It's not like you think!" Claire insisted, trying to wipe Sarah's face with the sticky paper that had been wrapped around her cone. "I didn't mean to—"

"Of course you did," Amandy hissed. "This is a *Massie* trick."

Claire gasped, her shocked expression betraying her. *How did she know that?*

"You e-mailed us the story, remember?" Sari sniffed back the tears. "You thought it was *sooo* funny how Massie spilled latte on Kristen's church dress because she thought it was too hideous for the dance, even though it was probably fine, but because it's *Westchester*, it just wasn't good enough or stylish enough or expensive enough or hot culture enough!"

"You mean *haute couture*?" Claire blurted. Then hated herself.

"I *knew* you changed." Amandy jumped off the dock. She shielded her eyes from the sun and scowled. "You've become totally EW!"

Claire knit her brow in confusion. *Extremely Wearable? Eternal Wannabe?*

"Extremely *Westchester*!"

Sarah and Sari jumped down and followed Amandy across the parking lot, rubbing their wounds and lick-rubbing their stains. Claire stood alone on the dock, her dress completely stain-free, feeling EW: Extremely *Worthless*.

Claire arrived at City Hall one minute past the official Kiss-Off starting time, and already there was a pastel-colored, fruit-scented, lip-glossed line that snaked out the door and down the concrete steps.

SAS were nowhere in sight.

What if they bailed because they didn't have anything to wear? Claire squeezed the tragic thought from her tortured conscience and hyper-prayed that wasn't the case. But she had no way of knowing. They had ignored her I-worked-ex-tra-hours-to-earn-dry-cleaning-money-for-you-and-I-am-so-be-yond-sorry messages for four days straight—just like Claire would have ignored Todd's had *he* tried to apologize for mess-ing up the dress sabotage. But the video he'd shot of SAS being ambushed was now a YouTube favorite. It had over fifty-nine thousand views and had scored 4.5 stars, so he had zero regrets.

Despite the overcast sky, the thick heat bore down on Claire like a soggy chenille blanket. *Or was that guilt?* A layer of sweat began forming under her flatironed bangs, and her Dress Barn dress might as well have been cut from sandpaper. Still, Claire was glad she'd worn it. Maybe it would show SAS that they were wrong about her. That she *hadn't* become EW

(Extremely Westchester) and that she was still very much EK (Extremely Kissimmee).

In front of her a busty woman wearing a tight, yellowing MISS KISS 1985 T-shirt was smoothing her palm over her daughter's side-part. The petite brunette held her breath and squeezed her blue eyes shut until the primal grooming session ended. Once it had, the mom leaned toward her daughter's pearl-studded ear and whispered something sage. Her thin lips seemed to be gobbling her daughter's curls like a hungry goldfish, while her wide brown eyes assessed the competition.

Behind Claire, a cluster of slightly older girls over-spritzed themselves with perfume samples they had probably swiped from the Beauty Boutique, while others sang songs from *High School Musical* to calm their nerves.

Standing amidst the feverish excitement, Claire felt like her heart was sinking in the Gulf of Mexico. She had waited her entire life to walk this line with her friends so they could support one another. Reassure one another. Hold hands and giggle in the face of competition. And, most important, dream about getting crowned Miss Kiss and touring the state for a glamorous year of mall openings, car shows, parades, wardrobe fittings, etiquette lessons, and image consultants.

Yet here she was, feeling ugly. Despondent. And alone.

Shuffling forward with the enthusiasm of someone boarding an overbooked flight to Siberia, Claire eventually inched her way inside. The usual wet-wood-meets-old-carpet smell of the municipal building had been temporarily masked by hair products, scented lip gloss, and body oils. Photos of mayors and presidents past had been removed, replaced with pink glitter–framed head shots of past winners dating back to 1990—an injustice that Miss Kiss 1985 teared up about the instant she noticed. A playlist of songs with the word *kiss* in them was crackling from the PA system, and peppy line monitors dressed in white overalls with red lip prints all over them clapped their hands and encouraged everyone to sing along. Currently, the selection was some oldie called "Your Kiss Is on My List." The moms sang while their daughters bit their nails and rolled their eyes in embarrassment.

An alligator-size check made out to Miss Kiss dangled by fishing line just behind the judges' table. The ONE THOUSAND DOLLARS printed out in red glitter-script reminded Claire why she'd spent the last eighteen hours solo-practicing her walk for her old Powerpuff beanies.

Just then a familiar burst of laughter came from the front of the line. It was a hearty mix of Amandy's cackle, Sari's pinched giggle, and Sarah's snort.

Without concern for the dozens of people ahead of her, Claire hurried past the giddy line monitors, waving her hand in an it's-okay-I-know-what-I'm-doing sort of way—a gesture that was lost on the other competitors.

"Hey, who do you think you are?" shouted a girl in a mint green taffeta gown.

"Um, there's a line, you know!" snapped a nursing mother whose free hand rested on top of her daughter's shoulder pad.

"Hey, isn't that the girl from *Dial L for Loser*?"

After that, no one said another angry word. Instead, the line of girls spit out their gum, stiffened, and smiled when she passed. Claire might have even smiled back had she not been terrified to make contact with SAS.

When Amandy saw Claire approach, she turned her back and twirled the loose piece of damp dark hair that had fallen from the side of her updo. Sarah and Sari turned too. Surprisingly, they were all wearing their Dress Barn dresses. Even more surprising, the dresses looked good as new.

"Hey," Claire said. But it sounded more like "ay" because her throat has stress-locked. "You guys look great," she said, meaning it. Sarah's wild curls had been smoothed into a ballerina bun, and Sari had pinned a giant red-felt heart to the side of her long blond waves. Each girl wore a slightly different shade of dusty pink shadow and her signature color glitter gloss. Self-tanner was evident from their flattering all-over glows, with the exception of Sari. Hers stopped abruptly at her jawline.

"I've been calling you guys." Claire tried to sound concerned instead of lonely and desperate.

"You and every other worldwide wastoid who saw us on YouTube," Amandy hissed, keeping her back to Claire.

The image of Todd getting bludgeoned by a laptop popped into Claire's mind. "I had *nothing* to do with that!" she insisted. "Pinky swear!"

Claire held out her baby finger, but SAS looked at it like it had just mined her left nostril.

Sari curled her lip. "We don't *do* that here."

Claire took back her pinky but refused to give up. "I worked extra hours to make enough money to get your dresses dry cleaned." She popped open her white Isaac Mizrahi for Target clutch and pulled out three ten-dollar bills.

"We got new ones," Sarah said flatly. "The manager of Dress Barn saw the YouTube video and felt sorry for us. She gave them to us for free so long as we mention the store if we win the pageant."

"Or decide to post another video on YouTube," Sari added with an "as if" eye-roll.

"That's great." Claire smiled more than she had to. "Still. You should take the money anyway and—"

"Claire Lyons? What are *you* doing over here?" asked a squat, jolly woman in a tone usually reserved for toddlers. Her black hair was blow-dried into a perfect bob, with the edges curled toward her rounded jaw. She was holding a copy of *Dial L for Loser* on DVD, consulting the photo of Claire to make sure it was really her.

"Yeah."Amandy smirked. "Aren't you supposed to be at the back?"

Sarah and Sari giggled into their costume jewelry–ringed fingers.

"No, dear." The woman hooked her plump fingers around Claire's thin arm. "You're not entitled to register at all."

SAS smirked, and flashes of blue, pink, and orange glitter reflected off their smug faces.

Claire's cheeks burned. She could feel everyone staring at

her. Did the whole town know what she and Todd had done? Was she being disqualified before she even signed up? Was Dr. Phil waiting for her outside?

"My name is Lorna Crowley Brown. I'm the pageant coordinator. And we would like you to be our local celebrity judge." She smiled, and Claire noticed a smudge of peach lipstick streaked across her front tooth. "We sent a formal request to your estate in Westchester. We assumed you had other engagements when you didn't respond. I have calls out to some up-and-coming twins from Clearwater, but we'd much rather have *you*."

"*Why?*" hissed Amandy. "Her movie was a flop."

Claire gasped. *This was getting dirty.*

"It closed after two weeks," Sari added.

"And was nicknamed *Dial S for Snoozer*," Sarah snickered.

Some of the girls in line giggled.

"You're making that up!" Claire stomped her foot.

"Well, it's been the number one rental over at Blockbuster on Golden Avenue for five weeks in a row," Lorna put in.

A few of the contestants began clapping their support. Claire smiled her thanks.

"What about *us*?" Amandy tried to silence the crowd. "Our YouTube video is way more popular!"

"Please say you'll do it." Lorna steepled her palms together in prayer, ignoring Amandy. "We would be *so* honored."

Claire faced the giant glitter check and bit her lower lip. It tasted like key lime pie–flavored gloss and confusion.

"Oh, and we offer a stipend," Lorna said with an encouraging eyebrow wiggle.

"A what?" Claire mumbled, just in case everyone else knew what that meant.

"A payment," Lorna mumbled back. She leaned toward Claire and lowered her voice. "Five hundred dollars."

SAS gasped.

"Really?" Claire's teeth started to chatter with excitement. It might not buy her a Westchester wardrobe, but five hundred dollars was certainly enough for a pair of jeans and *something* from the seventh floor of Barneys.

Claire turned to look at the hundreds of bright smiles urging her to accept this honor . . . three of which suddenly belonged to SAS.

From the curb, the Lyonses' house seemed peaceful, like it was enjoying a few moments to itself. Todd was blowing up baby pools for the neighbor's kiddie swim party. Judi and Jay were out running a "quick errand," which was code for, "We're at Dipper Dan's picking up a peanut butter ice cream cake to celebrate the big news," a sweet but somewhat tired family tradition.

Claire had been out riding her bike around the neighborhood to try to burn off her sadness as if it were a big slice of fattening cream pie and she was Massie. But "Lucky," the old Britney Spears hit, had been on a constant loop in her head since Lorna had asked her to be a judge. And that made her feel worse.

She's so lucky. She's a star. But she cry cry cries in her lonely heart. . . .

The song was about a famous actress who had everything a girl could ever want—except true companionship.

Granted, Claire was several Oscars away from "Lucky" status, but she could completely relate to the star's feeling of isolation. Being appointed a Miss Kiss judge was one of the biggest honors of her life, and she had no friends to celebrate with. She couldn't even brag to the Pretty Committee. To them, local pageants were about as glamorous as a McDonald's Playland. Unfortunately, this had struck her only *after* she agreed to be interviewed by the local news and four radio stations, one of which was FM. Hopefully the Blocks' satellite dish was down.

Claire coasted up the smooth black tar driveway and side-jumped off her pink and black bike. Despite an earlier triple-pit swipe of Secret Vanilla Chai, her dress was starting to smell like melting plastic.

For one billionth of a second she considered calling Cam with the news. Then, remembering how pointless that would be, she opted for Layne. She would send a link to the pageant's site with a message that said—

"SURPRISE!"

SAS jumped out from behind the blooming yellow rosebush by the front door.

"Ahhhhhh!" Claire slapped her hand against her heart, which was now pounding like someone trapped in a meat locker. "What are you guys doing here?" Her eyebrows shifted, shuffling through different emotions like a slot machine. Would they settle on surprise? Shock? Scorn? Finally, after seeing her smiling friends with errant leaves on their shoulders and thorny twigs stuck in their hair (Sarah!), Claire's expression landed on Pure Delight.

"Omigosh! We heard you on Kiss FM. It was so amazing and weird and awesome to hear your voice coming out the radio, which got me to wondering just exactly how that works, I mean I know there's this whole thing with waves and satellites but what does that really mean?" Sari reached into the inside square pocket of her pink cutoff sweat shorts and pinched out a few shelled BBQ sunflower seeds. "You want?"

"Sure." Claire smiled at Sari's signature word-vomit and opened her palm. Four warm seeds and a dusting of reddish brown seasoning landed softly inside, just like a peace offering should. She slapped them into her mouth. "Yummy."

"Here." Sarah held out her half-empty can of Dr. Thunder—the Dr Pepper rip-off that tasted almost exactly the same.

The lip of the can glistened with mint-flavored lip gloss, but Claire pretended not to mind one bit.

"Gummy?" Amandy shoved a crumpled white paper bag under Claire's chin.

"B's?" Claire asked, peering inside.

"They're lips," Amandy clarified. "Special edition in honor of the pageant. Every girl who qualified got a bag."

Claire helped herself to three.

"We already finished ours and ehmigosh, they were *so* good." Sari licked her thin lips.

"Wait. You're *in*?" Claire gushed with genuine enthusiasm. "You made it?"

"Yup!" Sarah busted out a spastic reverse shoulder-roll finger snap. "All of us!"

"While you were doing your interview for Disney radio, your best friends made it!"

So SACS were best friends again?

It was obvious times twenty that SAS was sucking

up to her because she was a judge. But it didn't matter. She'd thought she had lost them forever. This was her way back in.

"Listen, you guys," Claire said, putting her key in the lock. Her Coach-logo key chain (thanks, Massie!) knocked against the door. "I'm so sorry. I promise I won't act EW ever—"

"Lyons estate?" called the fuzzy UPS delivery guy with a snicker.

SACS turned around to find him pant-wheeling another giant wardrobe box up the driveway.

Claire felt her entire body redden.

"Looks like"—he consulted his black clipboard—"Maysee Flock is moving in."

Six eyeballs seared the left side of Claire's cheek.

"It's Mah-sseeee Block. And she's *not* moving in," she corrected, for SAS's sake. And hers. Then she scribble-signed her name beside the *X*, just like she had earlier on the official Miss Kiss welcome letter from the three pageant judges. Her fat, swirling script had looked funny between the sharp points of Vonda Tillman's signature (editor of the *Kissimmee Daily News*) and the wormy line of Mayor Reggie Hammond's. "Would you mind taking them upstairs? The room with the Hello Kitty stickers on the door."

"Butler's day off?" he cracked.

Claire smiled innocently at her friends, pretending she didn't hear him.

"What's *that* all about?" Sari asked, lifting her pointy chin to the thin man in brown shorts wrestling with a box a head taller than he was.

"Um, it's a surprise." Claire rocked back on the heels of her gold Michael Kors sandals, or *sand*-me-downs, as Massie called them. Then she shook her head. Would she ever be able to rid the alpha from her mind? Or would all thoughts lead back to her? It was like that old song she'd sung in kindergarten about the cat that kept coming back even though everyone thought he was a goner.

But how could she possibly focus on anything else when boxes of designer clothes were being overnighted to her doorstep? Was it Massie's way of telling Claire how much she missed her? Or letting her know she won't tolerate EW-fits in the eighth grade?

More than anything Claire wanted ten minutes to text the alpha and get some answers. But that would have to wait. Right now she had a bedroom filled with designer clothes and her three oldest friends standing by.

And both needed some serious attention.

"On the count of three, everyone push it to the bed." Claire pressed her palms against the wardrobe box, right next to the big purple letters that said, HANDLE W/CARE OR U WILL B SUED.

"Ready? One . . . two . . . threeeeee."

SAS added their hands to the box and the girls grunt-shoved the six-foot package across the white shag rug. It reminded Claire of last winter in Westchester when her dad had struggled for almost an hour to dislodge their Ford Taurus from a snowbank in the Bagel Paradise parking lot. She and Todd had stood outside in the cold, rubbing their hands together and cheering him on. Their words had come out in gray puffs, like they were smoke-breathing dragons.

The sudden memory surprised Claire. Now that she was tanned, barefoot, and swaddled in humidity, icy images like those should have been stored away until fall. But once again the scent of Chanel No. 19 was seeping through the corrugated crate and, like invisible ropes, dragging her back up the coast. It reminded Claire that leaving was entirely different than getting away.

She shook her head, focusing on the task at hand. When the box was in position, the girls climbed up on Claire's grass green bedspread and started attacking the seams.

"Use your nails!" Sari urged Sarah as she pounded the thick layers of clear packing tape.

"No way! I just painted them." Sarah wiggled her short, opalescent fingertips. They shimmered pink or pearly white, depending on their angle.

"I've got it." Claire plucked a pushpin from her daisy-covered headboard. The backward-facing photo of Cam seesawed to the floor. She stepped on it as she walked back over to SAS.

Now you know how I feel.

Using the pin, she poked at the packing tape until it tore into thin ribbons. SAS hungrily tore into the box of clothes.

"Omigosh!"

"These are amazing!"

"Look at this blue thang!"

Claire smiled while her friends dug through stacks of silk and margarine-soft cotton, trying to convince herself that she didn't mind the invasion one bit. But a tiny part of her would have preferred to be alone when the package arrived. Not because she didn't want to share, but because it would have been nice if she'd had the chance to take the more expensive pieces out. To protect them, of course.

"Why did she do this?" Amandy asked, her fists practically choking Chloé, Marc, and Calvin.

"Did you have to pay for them? Because if you did, I bet it's going to cost a lot. Not a lot like a-few-weeks'-allowance a lot. More like quit-school-and-work-full-time-for-your-brother a lot," Sari said, her upper body half in the box like a rat inside a boa constrictor.

"Do you get to keep them?" Sarah swayed back and forth with an electric blue pair of jeans. She accidentally knocked her hip on the corner of Claire's desk. "Owie!"

Normally everyone would have cracked up, even Sarah. But clothes were being tossed around the room like confetti. There was no time for distractions.

Claire watched the silk storm and wondered how to respond to their questions. The truth was that she wanted answers even more than they did. All she knew for sure was that since the box's arrival almost ten minutes ago, SAS hadn't once mentioned iced tea bombs, Westchester, or the Pretty Committee. The clothes were bringing friends and families together in ways that Santa only dreamed of.

"Massie sent this stuff for *all* of us," Claire fibbed. "You know, for Miss Kiss. She thinks its awesome you got in and she wanted to say congratulations."

"Beats flowers," Sarah said, gathering clothes off the floor.

"How thoughtful." Sari lifted her head out of the box. Her shoulders were draped with dresses.

"I knew she had to be cool if you were friends with her." Amandy tried to tilt-position a yellow knit beret over her damp brown hair, but it kept sliding off.

"Claire-Bear, you should totally take pictures of us in the clothes so we can e-mail them to her."

"Best idea ever! Even better than the time we decided to BeDazzle all our shoes and purses and belts and pants and pretty much everything." Sari pushed over the box like a raccoon digging through a trash can so she could get at the stuff on the bottom. She and Amandy jumped off the bed to greet it when it landed. "We can do our makeup and hair for the pictures, and—"

"We can shoot it at Publix so it looks like a real pageant!" Amandy said, crawling inside the box. "She'll love it!"

Claire's heart started to pound as she imagined Massie receiving a series of jpegs that featured SAS parading across a fish-scented loading dock in the clothes she'd sent just for Claire.

"Gotta pee." She casually grabbed her cell phone off the bed and raced out of the room.

Once inside the navy, nautical-themed bathroom, Claire speed-dialed Massie, knowing her questions were far too elaborate for a text. But the call went straight to voice mail. She tried again. And again. And—

Suddenly, "Pocketful of Sunshine" by Natasha Bedingfield blasted from her room. The call would have to wait.

Claire burst through the door. Then she gasped.

Amandy, Sarah, and Sari had piled on layer upon layer of clothes over their bodies. And now they were peeling them off and swing-tossing them around her room. Three-hundred-dollar cashmere tank tops were getting snagged on the corners of picture frames, delicate knit dresses were being broiled on lampshades, and a beautiful slip dress glided into Claire's metal mesh trash can. Claire's first instinct was to shut it all down and send everyone home. But the silly striptease *was* actually kind of funny. And whipping a tank top that cost more than an airline ticket across her room was something she'd never again have the chance to do. So Claire grabbed a stack of jeans out of the box and began giggle-pulling them on under her dress.

After the third pair—William Rast, dark wash—Claire began walking like the Tin Man. "Hey, guys, watch this!" But as she reached for a metallic gold scarf that was hanging off her desk chair, she lost her balance and crashed into Amandy.

"Ahhhhh!" The two toppled to the ground in fits of hysterics.

"Look out below!" Sarah and Sari began piling heaps of clothes on top of them like kindling on a bonfire.

"Man down! I'm trapped!" Claire's stomach ached as she lay beneath Amandy, laughing hysterically, her face smashed between the white shag rug and a Pucci tank. After several minutes of trying to wiggle free, Claire finally managed to extract herself from the Chanel-scented couture cave.

Right when she popped her head out, Sarah and Sari stopped giggling and "Pocketful of Sunshine" ended abruptly in the middle of the third chorus. Just like the frogs in the creek behind Claire's house stopped croaking when a larger animal was approaching, SAS became eerily silent.

"What's going on?" Claire turned her head and found herself face-to-leg with a pair of tanned, stubble-free, oil-slicked shins that were practically pressed up against her blond lashes. Suddenly, Claire's mouth tasted like pennies.

It was the Wicked Witch of Westchester. And her little dog too.

But judging by the burning rage behind Massie's amber eyes, this house call was about more than a stolen pair of ruby slippers.

Aside from the flared nostrils and hate-filled squint, Massie looked incredible. Dressed in silver lamé shorts, a skinny red crocodile belt, and a blousy ivory silk tank, she looked like a magazine cutout come to life. She was glossier than the rest of the girls in the room. Her coloring was richer, her textures more pronounced.

The whole thing seemed unnatural. Massie holding Bean against a backdrop of faded Hello Kitty stickers and girly home furnishings? It was like she was standing against one of those special-effects green screens, her edges more defined than the corny background's.

"Ohmygawsh, there she is!" Sarah speed-waved, then raced across the white shag toward Massie. "What an incredible surprise!"

Bean barked twice and Massie lowered her to the ground. She hurried under the bed to avoid getting trampled.

Claire forced herself to stand but couldn't move beyond that.

"You look exactly like you do in your pictures, except you're taller, obviously, and three-dimensional and totally nice and generous," Sari shouted, approaching from the left. "It's so nice to meet you. Gosh." Sari turned to Amandy. "Doesn't she look just like her pictures?"

"Better! I love your blond highlights. And that edgy purple streak behind your ear." Amandy hug-lifted the alpha.

Massie's arms clung stiffly to her sides. Her expression was cold and rigid.

"I *knew* it was a Westchester thang!" Sari declared as they wobble-placed her back down on the rug. "No one hugs up there, do they?"

Without a word, Massie quickly pulled a tube of Mango-MaGawd Glossip Girl out of her shorts and applied with life-and-death urgency. Her amber eyes darted back and forth, in synch with the lip wand, silently surveying the damage.

Why won't you speak? What are you thinking? Are you mad? How mad? If mad was a ten and not mad was a one, what would you be? Wait! Why are you even HERE???? Claire wanted to ask these questions and a billion more. But her tonsils held back the words like thick, protective arms, urging her to stand back and assess the danger before jumping in.

"You're shocked, right?" Sarah playfully knocked Massie on the arm. Her tanned skin flashed white for a second where Sarah had hit her. "You didn't think we'd like the EW clothes you sent us, did you?" She unzipped a lavender cashmere hoodie, revealing the black sheer blouse she'd stuffed underneath. "But we dooooo!" Tossing the hoodie on the floor like a used tissue, Sarah spun, lost her balance, then crashed onto the bed, creasing the front of the delicate black blouse.

SAS cracked up. Claire bit her thumbnail.

"It was super supportive of you to send clothes for Miss Kiss." Sari smiled, her top lip curling inward toward her gums.

SAS nodded in agreement. Claire gripped her stomach.

"I can't believe we ever thought you were *mean*." Amandy shimmied out of a True Religion miniskirt, revealing a pair of Massie's red and orange Cosabella boy shorts.

"I dunno if Claire told you this." Sari put her arm on Amandy's shoulder. "But *her* name used to be *Mandy* before she changed it to Ah-mandy. And Mandy sounds like Massie, which is kind of funny because you both have the same best friend and the same taste in clothes. I bet she could totally change it back if you wanted. So you could be more the same. Right?"

Amandy eagerly nodded yes.

SAS beam-grinned at Massie.

Slowly, Massie parted her high-glossed lips. Then she inhaled with a long, deep rattle that sounded like she was having an asthma attack. Unwittingly, Claire lifted her shoulders toward her ears. She clenched her teeth and squeezed her eyes shut, bracing herself against the force that was building inside of Massie. Preparing herself to face the eye of the storm. Hoping to—

"KUUUUHHHH-LAAAAAIRE!" Massie bellowed.

The pictures on the headboard fluttered. A Hello Kitty pencil rolled off the desk. SAS piled onto the bed and covered themselves with Claire's collection of DIY T-shirt pillows. Bean whimpered.

"So, um." Claire fanned her burning face and tried to smile. "What brings you to Orlando?" She giggled nervously.

"There's a cold front in the Hamptons." Massie sneered.

Suddenly, Claire remembered hearing something about

the Blocks taking a three-week luxury cruise in the Mediterranean and wondered if Massie had nowhere else to go. A teeny-tiny sympathy tingle, the size of a baby sea monkey, fluttered in her belly. She couldn't imagine her parents going away for three weeks and leaving her behind. But still. It was hard to feel 100 percent sorry for someone who made you feel unwelcome in your own bedroom.

"So if your FLBR friends wouldn't mind returning my stolen luggage and—"

"This is your *luggage*?" Amandy put her hand on her heart. "As in, the stuff you packed for *vacation*?"

Massie glared at her in an of-course-what-did-you-think-it-was? sort of way.

"Wow." Sarah pulled a candy necklace out of her back pocket and stretched it over her massive head of hair. "How long are you staying?"

Too long! Claire thought.

"What's an FLBR?" Sari asked, her voice slightly elevated by a hopeful lilt. "No, wait, lemme guess. Friends Love Bunny Rabbits." She turned to Massie. "Am I close?"

Massie stomped over to the bed, placed her hands on her hips, and glared down at the trembling SAS cluster. "It means you're a—"

"It means you're from Florida," Claire interrupted. "You know. Like you're my Florida friends." She sat on the edge of the bed, between Massie and SAS.

"What's the LBR part?" Sarah pulled her candy necklace toward her mouth and bit down.

Massie rolled her eyes. "Um, Claire, are you a locksmith?"

She shook her head no, desperately wishing she could mute the next five seconds of her life. Because someone was about to get insulted—probably her—and the last thing Claire wanted was for her Florida friends to see what Westchester was really like. Not that it was bad—just occasionally humiliating. And why make them worry?

"I asked, are you a locksmith?"

"No." Claire laughed, like this was a fun inside joke they shared.

"Then why are you hanging with these dorkys?"

Claire lowered her eyes in shame. *Did Massie really think her friends were so bad? And if so why wasn't Claire rushing to their defense?*

"Door *keys*?" Sarah scratched her head. "Why are we door keys?" She giggled.

"Maybe she means the *Florida* Keys," Sari tried. Then she turned to Massie with a compassionate smile. "Do you mean the Florida Keys? Because technically Orlando is part of the mainland. But the Keys are cool. Key West is super fun around the holidays."

Massie ignored her while she rearranged the headboard photos so that the shots of her were in the center.

Claire, feeling more in the middle than Malcolm, had the sensation that a giant gummy worm was wrapping itself around her heart. Either that or she was about to blow an artery. Like a superhero with the ability to read minds, she knew exactly what everyone was thinking. And the more tuned-in she became, the harder the gummy worm squeezed.

Undoubtedly, Massie was wondering why Claire was friends with these simple, unsophisticated girls. Girls who looked their age and saved their allowances for weeks just to buy one new thing at A&F. She probably assumed Claire was holding on to them for the summer because she had no one else. But now that *she* had arrived, it was okay to treat SAS like last season's flats.

And then there was SAS. They were probably thinking that Massie's icy attitude was just a New York thing, and that she would warm to them when she realized they had been officially accepted in the Miss Kiss pageant.

"We may be door keys." Amandy lifted herself up onto her knees on the edge of the bed and giggle-mumbled. "Whatever that means. But we are *grateful* door keys. Lending us your luggage for our pageant is—"

Claire braced herself for another storm.

"Pageant?" Massie practically spat. "Don't even *say* that word in front of my clothes. The sound alone is enough to make the fabric pill."

SAS's smiles faded to frowns. They finally got it.

"But"—Sari pout-glanced at Claire—"I thought you said these were gifts?"

"The only *gift* you're getting is a bill from my dry cleaner," Massie barked. "Now remove my clothes from your fruit-scented bodies before I—"

"Surprise!" Judi elbow-pushed the bedroom door open. Her

arms were shaking under the weight of an enormous peanut-butter ice cream cake in the shape of giant lips. "Everyone downstairs. We have a lot to celebrate!"

Suddenly Claire thought of the orchestra on the *Titanic* and how they started playing while the ship was sinking. Because celebrating, under the current circumstances, seemed just as pointless.

"Cake, cake, cake!" Todd chant-shouted as he bolted down the peach-carpeted stairs to the kitchen.

Jay Lyons was already seated at the head of the diner-style booth, anxiously slapping a pink plastic fork against the Minnie Mouse paper plate that was left over from Claire's eighth birthday party. Judi leaned over him, poking the frozen desert with letter candles that spelled W-E-L-C-O-M-E on the top lip for Massie and M-I-S-S K-I-S-S on the bottom for everyone else.

SAS slid in on one side of the booth, while Massie and Claire tucked into the other. Everyone pretended to be fascinated with Todd and his ability to run tight circles around the cooking island while screaming the word *cake* so they wouldn't have to look at one another.

Until today, the kitchen had been Claire's favorite room in the house. The booth, with its red sparkly vinyl padding and matching Formica tabletop, was not something most families were lucky enough to have. But Jay had won it at a church charity casino night and had decided to commit the entire kitchen to the 1950s soda shop theme.

The floor was covered in black-and-white tiles, and the appliances were the same ones that had belonged to Claire's grandparents. The blender was turquoise, and the Mixmaster was cupcake yellow. Pictures of old Cadillacs hung on the walls next to drawings of doting housewives pulling roasts from the oven. Two pairs of gray Reebok Rollerblades—ones her parents had been wearing when they first met—were preserved in a plastic shadow box beside the pantry. The room had more charm than *Juno*.

But now, Claire couldn't help seeing it all through Massie's amber eyes. And suddenly the whole theme thing seemed childish.

Just like her friends.

Claire wanted to hate Massie for making her feel this way. But couldn't. She had no one to blame for her insecurity tsunami but herself. Before Massie had arrived, she'd been proud of her hometown. Proud of its people. Proud of its pageants. *Gawsh!* Why did she always assume she had to *be* like Massie to be *liked* by Massie?

Claire grin-glanced at her FBFFs and made a silent promise: She was not going to let Massie Block influence her behavior toward them. Start-innnnnnnnnnnnnnnng . . .

. . . *now!*

"Remember the time we tried to set a world record by seeing how long we could sit under this table?" Claire giggled at the memory.

SAS smiled but did not lift their eyes.

"How long did you last?" Jay chuckled. "An hour?"

"More like two, Mr. L," Amandy giggled. "And it would have been longer if *he* hadn't thrown fire ants at us."

Todd proudly patted himself on the back, then sat on his father's lap. "You should have heard the screams!"

"We did!" Jay and Judi laugh-blurted at the same time.

"I started dialing nine-one-one before I even knew what happened," Judi reminded them.

Soon, everyone was cracking up. Claire's teeth chattered with joy.

"Sounds like a real YouTube moment," Massie mumbled, then flipped her hair. The pure essence of plants that was Aveda's signature scent temporarily eclipsed the peanut buttery smell of the cake.

Claire felt her smile wane. She was about to roll her eyes to show Massie that she too thought the whole ants-under-the-table thing was goofy. But wait! If Massie didn't like their idea of fun, she could leave.

"Hold on a minute, you're not going to spread this, are you?" Amandy quickly sobered.

"Huh?" Claire asked while her mother searched the kitchen drawer for matches.

"You know, you won't tell the other judges embarrassing stories about us, right?"

Claire knit her blond brows in confusion.

"Why aren't you denying anything?" Sarah leaned forward and covered her mouth in shock. "Is it because you already spilled?" She gasped and turned to SA. "She already spilled!"

"What are you talking about? I haven't even *met* the other judges yet."

"Aha! You said '*yet*.'" Sari pointed her finger in Claire's face. "But you're planning on it."

"Planning on *what*? On meeting them or telling them?" Claire looked at her father, hoping for a witness to the insanity. But he waved his hands like someone who didn't want to get involved.

Out of desperation, she glanced at Massie, but surprisingly, the alpha didn't have a single trace of an I-told-you-they-were-crazy-FLBRs expression on her face. Instead she was rubbing Chanel cuticle cream on her thumbnail. All traces of anger seemed to be gone. She looked serene—as if she hadn't just gotten abandoned by her parents and then sent to another state only to walk into a roomful of strangers parading around in her clothes.

"So, who are you gonna vote for?" Amandy fanned her face with the Minnie Mouse paper plate.

Claire opened her mouth to answer, then paused. She hadn't really thought about it.

"I met her first," Sari insisted. "'Member, Claire? We were gymnastics partners. I spotted you on the balance beam. I caught you when you started to wobble. It's almost like I saved your life."

"Yeah, but I was the first one to sleep at her house," Sarah insisted.

"Only because I had the chicken pox." Amandy pounded her fist on the Formica tabletop. "Thanks to *you*!" She pointed at Sari.

"Me?" Sari squealed. "I caught them from y—"

"What are they fighting about?" Massie asked quietly. "What *voting*?"

"Tell ya later," Claire mumbled back.

"Who wants cake?" Judi shouted over the shouting.

"Meeee!" Todd and Jay shouted.

"Here it comes," Judi announced as she placed the flaming ice cream cake in the center of the table. The letter-candles burned with the pride of an Olympic torch.

"On the count of three, I want Claire, Sarah, Sari, and Amandy to blow out the part that says MISS KISS. And Massie, you get the WELCOME part. Ready? One . . . two . . ."

"What do I get?" Todd whined.

"This." Claire slid her finger along the edge of the rectangular cake tray. She hooked a chunk of white icing and flicked it at her brother's face. It landed right on his nose.

"Claire!" Judi huffed, trying to look angry. But her pinched smirk gave her away.

Massie burst out laughing while Jay playfully licked it off his son's nose.

"Ew, Dad!" Todd giggled.

"Can I keep the MISS KISS candles, Mrs. L?" Amandy asked, completely ignoring the giddiness on the Lyonses' side of the table.

"No fair!" Sarah rubbed her curly blond hair. "I was going to ask."

"No, I was!"

"Why don't you blow them out first?" Judi tried to sound like she wasn't annoyed. "Before the ice cream melts."

"Fine," Amandy snapped. Then she leaned forward and blew.

"What happened to our three count?" Massie looked up at Judi, her amber eyes wide with innocence.

Judi shrugged while SAS began fight-pulling the candles.

"Um, is this full fat or low fat?" Massie smacked the lower lip of the cake with the back of her spoon.

"Is she serious?" Amandy asked, stuffing the *M*, *K*, and two *S* candles under her butt.

"Yeah, I'm serious," Massie huffed.

"Exactly how lame do you think we are?"

"Do you want me to answer that?" Massie scoffed, scooping up a piece of cake.

"Ha!" Todd shouted. He held out his hand so Massie could high-five it. But Jay pulled it down.

Claire stuffed a huge piece of cold peanut butter ice cream into her mouth and tongue-batted it around until it started to melt. It was either that or speak, and she had no idea what to say. No idea who to defend. No idea how her day had ended up this way.

Was it Miss Kiss pressure? The colliding of two worlds?

Or had everyone changed?

"We would *never* have *non*fat ice cream cake." Sari licked the side of her *I* candle. "How gross would *that* be?"

"Seriously gross," Amandy said, and Sarah agreed.

"Oh." Massie pushed her plate aside.

"How rude," Sarah murmured.

"Whatevs, I'm allergic to nuts, anyway," Massie said, digging through her makeup bag.

Claire recalled Massie eating Nutz Over Chocolate Luna bars on several occasions but decided this was not the best time to point that out. Her friends might have been feuding, but not with *her*. And she wanted to keep it that way for as long as possible.

"Oh yeah?" Amandy smoothed a finger over her thick brows. "What kind of nuts are you allergic to?"

Massie pulled a gold YSL compact from her makeup bag and held the mirror in front of SAS. "This kind!"

SAS huffed. Todd laughed. Jay and Judi focused on their cake. Claire didn't know whether to high-five Massie or book her on the next flight out. So she did what anyone who was caught in the middle of feuding friends would do. She downed another slice of full-fat cake, and when she finished it, she ate some more.

There was a certain feeling Claire got when Cam would gaze at her with his one blue and one green eye. It filled her with heat. Security. It made her believe she was special, even beautiful. And tonight, even though he was miles away *and* ignoring her, she had that feeling.

It was that perfect time of day when the sun was low but still shining. It cast an orange glow on the sides of the charming buildings in historic downtown and warmed people's cocoa-buttered skin like one last kiss before bedtime. On the stage inside Toho Square the local pop band Carbon Footprint began playing their upbeat hit, "Nature's Candy." Flip-flops flapped as fans pushed through the thickening crowd, racing to the grassy dance floor.

"Let's meet at the white press tent at"—Jay checked his black diving watch—"nine fifteen."

"'Kay." Claire bounced on the toes of the gold gladiator sandals Massie had insisted she borrow.

Judi leaned over and hugged her daughter. "Have fun, *judge*." She squeezed hard, enveloping Claire in the light scent of lilies and spearmint Dentyne Ice. "We're so proud of you."

"Thanks, Mom." Claire tried to wiggle loose. She felt like

a windup doll that was being held back, her insides all geared up to go.

"Don't party too hard." Todd straightened the red bow tie he'd insisted on wearing with his white T-Odd Jobs tank top and black surf trunks. "We have an early day tomorrow. Three lawns and a fish tank cleaning."

Claire rolled her eyes and grabbed Massie's arm, pulling her away from reality and toward the pink VIP carpet that led to the entrance.

Just like the guests, the iron "welcome" arch at the head of the outdoor recreation area had been highly decorated in honor of the special occasion. Red glitter covered the poles, and a plump pink balloon mouth hung between them. MISS KISS was written on the top lip, and KISS OFF was scrawled across the bottom. It was a bittersweet event that bid farewell to last year's winner and made room for this year's. Even though it wasn't for points, everyone in attendance knew the power of a first impression and had nicknamed the annual party accordingly.

"They call this the Miss *Butt* Kiss," Claire explained, adjusting her JUDGE sticker even though it was perfectly placed above the pocket on the sequined blue and red–striped Luella dress Massie had let her borrow for the occasion.

In a trillion years, she'd never imagined spending the Butt Kiss with an alpha from Westchester. Sarah, Amandy, and Sari were supposed to be by her side. The plan for the day had always been:

1. Morning tanning and playlist prep in Sarah's backyard.
2. Lunch at Sari's dad's restaurant. Pig out—it's on the house!
3. Get dressed at Amandy's (she has her own bathroom). Apply lucky glitter colors on the inside of wrists.
4. Photo session by Claire.
5. Get a ride into town from Denver, Sarah's hot stepbrother.
6. Smile-strut past the judges eight times (our lucky number).
7. Dance and size up competition.
8. Avoid judges when leaving so they don't see our sweaty bangs.
9. Begin hard-core prep for the pageant.

But after last night's social storm, Claire thought it might be better to keep everyone separated, just for now. And since she wasn't competing and didn't *have* to look perfect for the party, it kind of made sense.

Surprisingly, SAS had understood. When they'd all met this morning, they had told her they'd respect her boundaries now that she was a judge and assured her that they'd give Massie a second chance. They'd even promised to set a place for her at their pig-out lunch so she could be there in spirit; otherwise they'd miss her too much. In return, Claire had vowed to help them buy makeup for the pageant. So what if that was against contest rules? She was their *best* friend. It was to be expected. And that's exactly what she told them. The promise had been enough to mend the hairline fracture in their friendship, seal in the love, and keep the peace. For one more day, at least.

"Ehmagawd, is that Rory Gilmore?" Massie tightened the purple men's tie she had threaded through the belt loops of the black satin shorts she'd paired with a matching vest. She was the only one in attendance wearing the forbidden color, and she seemed to delight in the drive-by glares she was getting from the Pastel Posse (as she called them).

Like a manatee in a sun shower, Claire let the comment slide off her back. So what if her home had a small-town vibe? It was charming. Festive. Spirited. Warm! And maybe, if Massie just gave it a chance, she'd appreciate it too.

"Claire?" Lorna Crowley Brown appeared in front of her, wearing a loose white blouse covered in DIY lipstick kisses from her own heart-shaped mouth. She had tucked the shirt into white capri jeans that fit snugly over her pear-shaped bottom. "Here is your rulebook." She handed Claire a red leather–bound binder filled with dividers and serious pages. "There is a section called Fairness Over Friendship. I suggest you read it thoroughly." Her narrow green eyes bored into Claire's. "And try to limit your mingling tonight to the other judges."

"Of course." Claire held the notebook close to her heart. It smelled like roses.

Lorna placed her plump hand on the small of Claire's back.

"Now, if you wouldn't mind walking the pink carpet so the press cameras could take your picture . . ."

"Of course," Claire said, like this happened to her every day. But on the inside she was doing that thing where you jump and click your heels together.

Finally, Massie would see that *she* was an alpha too.

"Claire Lyons! Judge and star of *Dial L for Loser*," Lorna announced to the press who were corralled behind BeDazzled stanchions.

They lifted their cameras and began clicking. The onslaught of attention gave Claire a bit of nervous tunnel vision. The music and party chatter sounded garbled. Muted. Underwater. If not for the crisp scent of Chanel No. 19, she would have had no idea that Massie was right beside her.

Sneaking a side peek, she caught the alpha coyly twirling her purple hair streak and posing with hand-on-hip confidence.

"What magazines are these guys from?" she managed through a frozen smile and clenched teeth.

"Mostly local papers and a few schools," Claire muttered through the corner of her mouth.

The perfume scent was instantly gone. Massie ducked under the lenses of the cameras and hurried inside to the party.

"Welcome, Judge Lyons. My name is Gracie. Don't you look beautiful this evening?" A perky redhead wearing a dusty pink gown covered in purple flowers approached Claire at the end of the carpet and gave her a tall lemonade. "Thirsty?"

Claire accepted the frosty glass graciously. If Massie had

still been there, Claire would have winked and mouthed, "Butt kiss."

"It's an honor to have you here. I loved your movie. My name is Gracie—oh, I already told you that, didn't I? I'll be competing on Saturday. I've been rehearsing nonstop, and I'm really hoping there's a dance round." She eyed Claire's judge's notebook. "I think I'll really shine in that."

"You're off to a great start." Massie came up behind Gracie, sipping a bottle of Perrier. "You may want to consider some pressed powder on your T-zone. It's oily times ten."

"Darn Proactiv!" Gracie's green eyes fluttered as she frantically palmed her face.

Claire gasp-dragged her friend away. "Thanks for the lemonade," she called to Gracie. "And good luck on Saturday."

She pulled Massie through the dense crowd toward the band, trying her best to return the friendly smiles she encountered along the way without appearing to be choosing any favorites.

In the distance, near the dunking booth, SAS were slowly and stiffly walking past Vonda Tillman, editor of the *Kissimmee Daily News*–slash–Miss Kiss judge, trying to make their first impression.

Claire giggled and steered Massie to an empty corner behind the stage. Once they were safely surrounded by noncompeting dancing guests, Claire would work up the nerve to give Massie a lecture on respecting her town and the people who lived in it. But when she saw the wood steps of the stage—the stage where she would be seated in less than a week—Claire touched her heart and sighed. "I can't believe I'm a *judge*." Her wide blue eyes seemed to look through the bobbing musicians and fix on an imaginary scene. "Do you know what an *honor* this is?"

"Yes, *your* honor." Massie smirked. Her teeth looked extra white against her bronze skin.

"There's our best friend!" Amandy had abandoned trying to impress Vonda and was now elbowing her way past Massie to throw her arms around Claire.

Sari and Sarah danced up as well, subtly nudging Massie to the outside of their circle.

Claire checked to make sure Lorna was at a safe distance before she acknowledged them.

"Wow, you guys look ah-mazing!" Claire whisper-blurted. She had tried not to talk like the Pretty Committee while she was with SAS, but after spending all day with Massie, gossiping about the people back home, it just kind of happened.

"Do you think we made a good first impression?" Sarah twirled on her heel. Her mint green halter dress spun around her calves, and orange glitter specks fell from her wrists like fairy dust. Sari was wearing the same dress in peach, with pink wrist glitter, and Amandy had accented her lavender dress with blue wrist glitter. They looked like a new girl group fixing to take the stage after Carbon Footprint.

"Those dresses remind me of grocery store cupcakes," Massie stated flatly, making it hard for the girls to be certain if it was a compliment or an insult.

"Your outfit reminds me of a biker funeral," Amandy hissed.

"Well, your eyebrows—I mean, *eyebrow*—reminds me of a—"

"We're going to take a short break!" announced the black-haired lead singer as he wiped his forehead with his peace-sign sweatband.

The dancers moaned their disappointment, then shuffled off in search of beverages, leaving Claire and her illegal conversation exposed.

"So what are this year's rounds?" Sari reached for the red leather binder.

Quickly, Claire ducked behind a tall speaker. "I can't tell you that now. It's against the rules," she whisper-shouted. "I can't even be seen with you."

"Makes sense to me." Massie smirked at Amandy.

"And what makes *you* so special?" Sari asked in her most nasal voice.

"DNA," Massie fired back.

Claire leaned against the speaker, closed her eyes, and shook her head like a weary parent.

"Well, your DNA wouldn't even get you past the first round of Miss Kiss," Sari huffed.

Claire bit her other thumbnail.

"Um, Scary?"

"It's *Sari*."

"Not only would I make it past the first round, I'd win."

Claire's heart began to pound. She closed her eyes. She didn't have to see the alpha to know where this was going.

"You have to be a local to enter," Amandy stated.

"I'll use Kuh-laire's address."

"You have to have talent," Sarah tried.

"I *am* talent."

"The contest is closed." Sari insisted.

"I don't think that will be a problem."

What?

Claire peeked out from behind the speaker. Massie was storming through the crowd heading straight for Lorna Crowley Brown.

"Is she serious?" Amandy knit her thick brows.

Claire wanted to answer *yes!* but was too mortified to speak.

Massie broke up a conversation between Lorna, a dad, and some young hopeful wearing a tiara and a mini sash that said, FUTURE MISS KISS.

Massie tilted her head to the side, projecting sweet sincerity. But Lorna shook her head no.

"Ha!" Amandy blurted.

Claire breathed a sigh of relief. She was already caught between Massie and SAS. Imagine having to make it official by casting votes! The thought alone made her intestines twist and turn into what felt like a big skull and crossbones. DANGER, indeed.

Instead of turning on her kitten heel and marching back, Massie twirled her purple hair streak around her finger. Lorna's eyes widened. She ran her hand through her black blowout, then made a quick call on her cell.

Seconds later they shook hands.

SAS shook their heads.

And Claire just shook.

The three-and-a-half-hour limo ride from Orlando to Miami was still not enough to vanquish the moldy smell of Mrs. Crane's fish tank from Claire's nostrils. A shower would have helped. Or the chance to change out of her denim cutoffs and sweat-stained tee, but Massie and her hired driver had stalked the T-Odd Jobs crew from house to house, begging them to hurry so Massie could go shopping.

On the endless ride, Massie shared stories of her short career as a top seller at Be Pretty cosmetics, while Claire nodded like someone who was listening. Instead, she was try-ing to figure out a way to judge the Miss Kiss pageant *and* keep her friends.

Finally, the limo turned onto Kendall Drive.

". . . It turns out the LBRs weren't beyond repair after all. Because I was turning threes into eights, fives into nines, and eights into tens. And it wasn't that hard. Just a little con-structive criticism and ah *lot* of makeup." Massie checked her gloss in her YSL compact.

At first, the mere mention of numbers sent Claire's teeth straight for her longest nail. How could she possibly give one of her friends a higher score than another?

". . . So on average I turned every LBR into an eight, at

least. . . ." Massie flicked a random piece of gold glitter off her purple and white–striped slouchy tunic.

That's it!

And just like that, Claire had her solution. She'd give all of her friends eights. Then she wouldn't have to choose between them. And eight was their lucky number, so . . .

Problem solved!

She wanted to lean across the shiny black leather interior and hug-thank Massie for the inspiration. . . .

But wait . . .

How could she possibly give Massie and Amandy the same score in the Beauty round when Amandy's brows looked like bangs? How could she give Sari an eight in the Speed Question-and-Answer round when *her* answers took *days*? And how could she make anyone with working eyes believe that Sarah's "Physical Interpretation of a Serious World Issue" wasn't intended to be a slapstick comedy?

"How did you *make* them eights if, you know, they were, say, threes?" Claire asked Massie as they stepped out of the limo in front of the department store.

"Easy." Massie turned and wagged her iPhone, indicating to the driver that she'd call when they were done. "I told them the truth."

"Which was?"

"Which was, 'You're ugly, but don't worry, because I can help.'" Massie charged past the throngs of salespeople threatening to sample-spritz them with the new fall perfumes. "Hurry!"

Massie grabbed Claire's arm and pulled her to the safety of the elevators. As soon as the doors closed behind them, she pressed her nose into Claire's white blond hair and inhaled. "All clear."

She held out a handful of her glossy brown hair. "Me?"

Claire leaned in and sniffed for perfume. "They got you." She waved away the light scent of flowers.

Normally she would have lied to the alpha, just to keep her in a good mood. But she had a lot of truth-telling to do in the next week and needed all the practice she could get.

Massie pulled her hair to her nose. "Marc Jacobs. Daisy. It's fine."

Claire smiled to herself. She could do this . . . so long as Lorna Crowley Brown didn't find out.

The floor Massie chose was filled with starved manne-quins looking glamorously blasé in the new season's crop of designer wear. The colors were bright and the—

"Done!" Massie announced.

"What?" Claire giggled. "Already?"

"Yup." She held up a black silk V-neck Geren Ford dress with ruching down the front. "It's perfect."

And it was. For New York City cocktail parties or front-row seats at fashion week. But not for Miss Kiss. The shiny black silk with its plunging neckline and rib-hugging pleats did not say, *I'm a fresh, innocent flower who would be honored and humbled to represent Kissimmee, Florida, and act as a mentor for your young daughters and troubled youth.* It said, *I'm bringing SexyBack.*

And in order for Claire to make her friends EW (EightWorthy), she'd have to toughen up and attempt the impossible. She'd have to give Massie Block clothing advice.

"How about this one?" Claire held up a dusty rose dress made of soft jersey material. Its floor-length skirt was comprised of three tiers, the third of which looked like satin. "It's Theory!" she announced, knowing Massie had a soft spot for their sweaters.

"It's *pink*!" Massie jumped back as if it were somehow contagious.

"Listen." Claire whisper-searched the perimeter as she inched toward Massie. "As a judge, I'm not allowed to give advice to Kiss competitors, but since it's you, I'll—"

"Since it's *me*, you'll give me the best score no matter what, *right*?" Massie threw the black dress over her shoulder.

"I can't just do that." Claire hung the Theory back on the rack. "It has to look believable. And no one is going to believe I gave you a high score if you wear *that*."

"Why nawt?" Massie took a step toward the register.

"Because," Claire huffed, "it doesn't say Miss Kiss. It says Miss Thang. And that's not what this pageant is about."

"So you're saying to be a good role model I have to look bad?"

"No." Claire suddenly felt like crying. Why couldn't Massie understand that Claire was trying to help? "Why do you want to be in the Miss Kiss anyway?" she blurted. "You've been making fun of it ever since you got here."

"Because I want to win." Masse rolled her eyes like it should have been obvious.

Before Claire had a chance to respond, her cell phone vibrated. She turned her back on Massie to read the text.

Sarah: Denver can drop us at your house now. Ready?

Claire's skin prickled with heat. Her heart revved. Her hands dampened. How could she have forgotten? She'd promised SAS she'd help them buy pageant makeup. Even if she left now, she wouldn't be home until dinnertime.

Her eyes scanned the store. Massie was by the cash register digging through her white Juicy Couture Alpha handbag, clearly in search of her wallet. Claire wondered what Massie would do in a situation like this. But the answer was obvious. She would *never* be caught between two groups of feuding friends, trying to please everyone.

Massie simply wouldn't care.

Claire: Stuck on a job until 6 pm. Can we go tomorrow?

After a long pause, Sarah finally responded.

Sarah: Fine. But SHE better not be there.

Claire snapped her rhinestone-encrusted cell closed.

"You ready? I could use a latte." Massie hooked her shopping bag over her shoulder and pulled Claire over to the escalator. "Tomorrow let's try to find a decent spa."

Claire eyed the overflowing tissue paper in Massie's Saks bag with contempt but flashed her most agreeable smile. She had the long drive back to learn how to tell the truth . . . or dream up her next big lie.

Massie rolled down the window of the limo and poked her head out. Bean hopped onto her lap and rested her chin on the window frame. "Remind me again why you have to work?"

Claire waved to her next-door neighbor, Mrs. Bower, who was peering through the hedges, wondering why a black stretch was parked in the Lyonses' driveway.

"I have to work to make money," Claire said, like they had been through this a thousand times.

"How about I pay you to come with me?" Massie adjusted the air-conditioning vent so that it blew on her face.

"Todd needs me," Claire lied. The truth was, she'd paid him twenty dollars to let her take the day off and not tell Massie. "Some woman hired us to go through her trash and pull out all of the recyclables. It's gross, but she's a regular client so—"

"So you'll be here when we get back?" Massie scratched behind Bean's ears.

"Pinky swear."

They shook.

Claire handed the driver an address through his open window, which he immediately entered into his GPS. It was for Kim's Global News & Sundries—a well-stocked international newsstand in Tampa that sold papers and magazines from all over the world. Somehow Claire had managed to convince Massie that she would have a leg up in the Physical Interpretation of World Events round if she interpreted a world event that Americans knew nothing about. There were a couple of local shops with the same international papers, but Claire needed all the Massie-free time she could get. And Kim's was two hours away.

Minutes after the limo pulled away, SAS appeared on Claire's doorstep. They were dressed in identical black-and-blue Orlando Magic tank tops and tight black short shorts.

"What are you wearing?" Claire giggle-asked as she pulled them inside and quickly shut the door.

"Our Halloween costumes." Sarah slapped her hands on her hips like a cheerleader, but somehow the gesture looked more angry teacher. "You told us to come in disguise."

"I meant be discreet so no one would notice you," she teased, leading the way up the peach-carpeted stairs. "This is a little obvious, don'tcha think?"

"Don't worry," Sari began. "Denver dropped us three blocks away like you asked. You know, right on the corner of Brooks and Carriage Lane. Next to the big house with the sunflowers and that cute porch swing. You guys should get a porch swing. No, wait—you're moving. Gosh! I can't believe you're moving. For good this time, too. It's so—"

"Where's Massie?" Amandy interrupted as they entered Claire's room.

"Shopping. I told her I wanted to spend the day alone with you guys."

"And she was fine with that?" Amandy said to the purple Scandia Down duvet on Claire's bed.

"Yeah. Of course." Claire sat on her own green comforter, which had been moved to the AeroBed blow-up mattress against the wall. The air mattress popped up on either side like a giant U when Sari sat beside her.

"What's that?" Amandy pointed to the round purple velvet pillow that had been clamped to the side of the bed. It looked like a motorcycle's sidecar.

"It's for the dog." Claire snickered, knowing how ridiculous it all must have seemed.

"Aren't you allergic?" Sarah asked.

Claire's belly filled with warmth. She remembered.

"I got a prescription." Claire sniffled.

Amandy slid into the middle of Massie's puffed-up bed, leaving a trail of blue wrist glitter in her wake. She rolled over to the side table and spritzed the lavender sheet spray, then put the satin sleep mask over her eyes and folded her hands over her chest like a corpse. "Ahhhhh." She kicked her white flip-flops to the floor, introducing her bare feet to the joy of high thread-count sheets. "Is this silk?"

"I wanna feel." Sarah dove on top of Amandy. Orange glitter fell off her wrists and mingled with the blue.

"Uh, Rihanna, anyone?" Claire hurried to her computer and cranked up "Don't Stop the Music." If that didn't get them off Massie's bed, nothing would.

Seconds later the girls were dancing and singing like a regular bunch of friends who weren't days away from competing for the biggest prize of their lives.

Do you know what you started?

I just came here to party.

During a half spin, Claire caught Sari hovering over her desk, flipping through the Miss Kiss Judges' binder. Her butt was shaking to the beat while her head hung over the pages.

"What are you doing?" Claire grabbed the binder. "That's illegal."

That same feeling of betrayal she'd had at Saks welled up inside her again—although this time it was mixed with the feeling of being taken advantage of.

"I bet Massie's seen it," Sari snapped, pulling at the elastic waistband of her skirt.

"She has *not*," Claire insisted, finally telling the truth.

Amandy lowered the music. "And we're supposed to believe that?"

"You can believe anything you want." Claire tossed the binder in her underwear drawer and slammed it shut.

"I believe her," Sarah said with a peculiar glare. A glare that seemed to remind Sari and Amandy of an earlier discussion. A glare that said, *Stay on track and don't mess this up.*

"Sorry." Amandy stepped forward and placed a chilly hand on the shoulder of Claire's red T-Odd Jobs tee. "We don't want you to do anything that makes you uncomfortable, Claire-Bear."

"She's right," Sari admitted, biting her thin lower lip.

"You're already doing so much to help us. And I bet you'll do even more when it comes time to vote, so—"

Amandy elbowed her in the rib. Hard. Sari pretended it didn't hurt.

Claire didn't need a brain to know she was being used. The sudden I'll-never-be-able-to-swallow-food-again feeling would have told her. But could she blame them? If she had never moved to Westchester and had never been asked to judge, would she be like SAS and do anything to win the Miss Kiss?

With that in mind, Claire highlight-deleted the last five minutes from her mind and decided to start fresh.

"Let's get started," she announced.

The girls lined up in front of her like obedient soldiers. But instead of screaming like a drill sergeant, Claire whispered like an informant.

"What I'm about to tell you is classified information. It may be painful at times, but it's for your own good. So listen up."

They nodded silently, communicating that they were ready to do whatever was necessary to beat the competition—and one another.

"Let's start with the Beauty round," Claire said. "The judges will be looking for fresh, girly, and fun. Sarah, that means the only thing in your hair should be deep conditioner. No good luck charms, no gum. If anything accidentally falls out, it could be devastating to your score."

Sarah wrote everything on her hand.

"Oh, and make sure your wash that off," Claire insisted.

"Do me!" Sari clapped.

Claire inhaled for strength. "I suggest buying some lip plumper. This *is* Miss Kiss and you *will* get judged on your cement lip print. If we only see lower lip and teeth, it will work against you. You have to get that top lip to show up. Got it?"

"I do! I'll get that Lip Venom stuff and I'll rub pepper on it, because I heard that swells lips. Maybe if I rub my bottom teeth against it for, like, the next few days it will get swollen and—"

"Sounds like a plan." Claire smiled. "Now Amandy." She sighed, knowing this wasn't going to be easy.

"I know, I know, dry my hair." Amandy twirled a damp dark strand around her pale finger. "Don't worry, I'm getting a blowout Friday night and I'm going to sleep sitting up."

"I'm hoping that will help us see your eyes more," Claire eased into it. "They are so expressive and that goes a long way with judges."

"Really?" Amandy's face lit up.

"Yeah, I'm just trying to think of how we could get an even better look at them. Maybe some mascara, or shadow." Claire tapped her index finger against her lip.

"How about an eyebrow wax!" Sarah blurted.

Sari burst out laughing.

"What's wrong with my eyebrows?" Amandy petted them like lost kittens.

"Nothing if your name's Bert and you live on Sesame Street," Sarah joked.

"My whole family has these brows," Amandy whined.

"Well, my whole family has *this*." Sarah pointed to the mall bump on the bridge of her nose. "But I'm still getting rid of it the day I turn twenty-one."

Amandy glared at Claire with moist eyes, silently asking if this was valid. With compassion and kindness, Claire slowly nodded. "The salon has an aesthetician. Make an appointment when you get the blowout. You won't regret it."

"Fine." Amandy leaned her head forward so that her hair fell over her face.

"I know how you feel." Claire reached for her friend's hand. "Believe me."

Amandy pulled away and folded her hairy arms across her chest. Claire decided to hold back on the arm wax suggestion for now. Maybe later in the week she'd suggest a cute gown with long sleeves.

For the next hour Claire tried to teach Sari how to get to the point when answering the Speed round questions by pinching her. With every passing second she'd tighten her grip, forcing Sari to answer quickly. After several tries and many tiny bruises on the back of her arm, she was able to sum up her biggest fear in three words: "My mother's thighs."

The Interpretative Dance round started smoothly. Amandy did a great job of showing the effects of global warming by prancing gaily like a deer in love. Then, as her medley of classical songs took a dark and stormy turn, she began stomping like acid rain, thrashing like tidal waves, and choking like the earth's innocent inhabitants. Then she spiraled to her death like she was sliding down a giant corkscrew. It was an eight-worthy EW.

Next, Sari tackled celebrity teen drug and alcohol addiction, set to a medley of Britney Spears songs. It started with "Stronger," peaked at "Oops, I Did It Again," and ended with "Toxic." The routine was loaded with several of Britney's signature dance moves and might have come off as more of an extended music video. But if you really focused on the lyrics, it made a major statement about the sad state of chemical dependency among the overprivileged.

Finally, Sarah stepped onto the white shag rug. "Flight of the Bumblebee" by Nikolai Rimsky-Korsakov buzzed from Claire's iPod dock while Sarah ran around the room in circles flapping her arms. After a few laps she started to get dizzy and began wobbling into the furniture. Then she lifted up on her tippytoes and raised her arms above her head, the way a little girl in a ballet recital would play a blooming flower. But she lost her balance and crashed into the AeroBed.

Claire turned off the music.

"What are you doing?"

Sarah steadied herself on the headboard. "I'm interpreting the whole bee crisis. They're dying off, you know. And that will totally affect our food and flower supply."

"Um, I think the scientists solved that," Claire fibbed.

"Seriously?" Sarah stood, her shoulders hung forward in defeat. "How am I going to learn a new routine by Saturday?"

Claire looked at her ceiling fan like she was thinking, even though the solution to this problem had come to her at four in the morning. "I know!" She looked at Sarah with renewed hope. "Why don't you interpret the recent study that claims California will get hit by a major earthquake in the next thirty years."

"How would I do that?" Sarah pulled a pen out of her hair and held it above her open palm.

"It's easy." Claire took the pen and tossed it over her shoulder. "Just shake and jiggle and crash into things."

"In other words," Amandy hissed, "be yourself."

"Easy, Bert!"

"Stop calling me that!" Amandy jumped off Massie's bed, ready to fight.

Kuh-laire . . . Kuh-laire . . . Kuh-laire . . .

Claire flipped open her cell phone.

Massie: Five minutes away. Ah-mazing store! Spent $300 on Euro fashion mags. U back yet?

Had it been four hours already?

Claire: Yup.

She snapped her cell shut. "Everyone out! Lorna Crowley Brown is down the street and wants to stop by."

"Why?" Amandy peered outside.

"She, um, wants to add some pages to my binder."

"What about my new routine?" Sarah pouted.

"You'll be fine. We have all week to practice. You're a natural."

"You can say that again," Amandy snickered.

"Why, are you *deaf*?" Sarah snapped. "Did your eyebrows grow into your ears?"

"Stop!" Sari shouted.

"That's the shortest thing you've ever said," Sarah blurted.

Sari opened her mouth to respond, but Claire slapped her hand over it.

"Trying to give me a fat lip?" she mumbled.

"What? No!" Claire insisted. "I'm trying to keep you guys from killing each other. It's only a contest. It's not worth it."

Sari pulled Claire's hand away. "Then why are you kicking us out?"

Claire sighed, wishing she had a speedy answer. But Massie was minutes away and the truth would have taken too long. So she held her door open and hugged her friends goodbye as if nothing between them had changed.

Outside, in the center of Toho Square, the pulsating theme song to *American Idol* started playing in Claire's head the second Lorna escorted her to the pink judges' table. Claire was seated on the far left—or Randy Jackson's side, as she liked to think of it. Vonda Tillman, the tall and tanned editor of the local paper, had Paula's famed middle seat, and stocky Mayor Reggie Hammond was on the far right, Simon style. Like on the TV show, the judges had been placed at the foot of the stage. They sat with pink pens poised, ready to shatter dreams, while spirited audience members waved banners behind them and a string quartet played soothing classics from the Baby Einstein CDs.

But despite the musicians' attempts to ease the mounting tension, Claire could hear the frantic clack of the contestants' unsensible shoes scuttling against the wood as they scurried behind the bloodred velvet curtain, trying to perfect themselves during these last few minutes before showtime. The press, which was clustered to Claire's right, was only adding to the pageant frenzy. She could feel the anticipation drip off their bodies as they cocked their cameras, ready to click away in case a catfight erupted.

Or was it sweat?

At sunrise the temperature had already hit eighty-seven degrees. Now that it was noon, it must have been over one hundred. Claire couldn't imagine spending the morning with a flatiron or hot curlers, trying to put makeup on a slick, flushed face, or squeezing swollen feet into stiff leather stilettos. Nor could she imagine pacing backstage, trying not to bite her nails, knowing that she was minutes away from competing against her best friends.

So what if she never got to fulfill her fantasy of becoming Miss Kiss? Judgeship was far better. She was wearing a white cotton sundress and Keds, her hair was in a high pony, and she had nothing on her face but SPF 30 and peach lip gloss. Best of all, she was sitting beside a turbo-industrial fan with the cool, relaxing knowledge that at the end of the day she'd be five hundred dollars richer.

"Five minutes," Lorna Crowley Brown announced from a podium on the far left of the stage. The quartet began one last tea-party favorite while the crowd roared as if gearing up for a jousting match.

"Please take your seats so we can begin." Lorna beamed with excitement. Today, the bottom of her black bob had been curled away from her jaw like the letter J; it bounced around her chin as she hurried to gush-greet Brenda and Billy, the local news's anchor team.

"Does anyone have a tissue?" Mayor Reggie leaned across the table and lifted his sunglasses. His dark eyes were flooded.

"Allergies?" Vonda asked, rummaging through her Miss Kiss gift tote.

Mayor Reggie chuckled and looked slightly embarrassed. "Emotions, I'm afraid. This is the last year I'll be judging."

"Why?" Claire blurted, shocked. He had been a fixture of the pageant for as long as she could remember. He was their Simon. Only nice. And bald. And American.

"Next summer my best friend's niece will be old enough to enter," he said with pride. "I'm just not sure I could be impartial. And that wouldn't be fair to the other hopefuls. So…" He sighed and accepted a crumpled mint green tissue from Vonda with a gracious smile.

Claire gulped, her mouth tasting like quarters. If the mayor had any idea how she'd spent the last week, he'd run her out of town:

Wednesday she'd gone to Sephora with SAS and helped them pick out makeup by hinting-suggesting they buy tropical sea shades only, since that was the color palette the judges were told to favor.

Thursday she'd met SAS at Publix to help make their walks EW. And yesterday, she'd spent five hours coaching their interpretative issues dances in the storage room of Sari's father's restaurant.

To be fair, Claire had offered Massie the same (illegal) services. But, like a true alpha, Massie had refused.

"Do you aw-nestly think I need help beating these people?" she'd asked with the utmost sincerity. "I hate to brag, but this is kind of like putting Gisele on *America's Next Top Model* and asking if she needs any pointers."

Massie was right, of course, but Claire knew that so long

as she insisted on wearing earth-tone makeup and black cocktail dresses, it was anyone's pageant.

"Eh-chem." Lorna cleared her throat into the microphone the way someone does when they want the crowd to stop talking.

Claire bit her pinky nail as she waited for the cheering to settle to chatter and the chatter to subdue to an occasional cough. She didn't know what she was more nervous about— her friends or her friend*ships*.

Finally, the crowd went silent. Lorna lifted the mic to her pink lips and smiled widely at the audience. A light breeze danced across the stage, but Lorna's *J*'s stayed stiff.

"For seventy-five years, the Miss Kiss pageant has given young girls an opportunity to harness their potential and engage in friendly, supportive competition. So friendly, in fact, that it has fostered many lifelong friendships and . . ." Lorna paused while the audience snicker-mumbled about how off the mark she was. "A-nnnnd I am honored to present this year's crop. A group so polished, talented, and professional that MTV decided *not* to put them on a reality show, because there was no drama." She lifted her palm as if swearing in a court of law. "As many of you know, the pageant is broken up into three rounds. First, our twenty lovely competitors will take the stage for the Speed Question-and-Answer round. After that, only five Kisses will be left standing, and—"

"GO KYLEE!" a man shouted, pumping his fist in the air.

A group in the back began cheering. "Beth! Beth! Beth!"

"PEYTON RULES!" yelled a woman with an unfortunate perm.

"SUUU-ZEEEEEE!" hollered a gaggle of young girls in the front row.

High-pitched screams followed, and soon the entire audience was lifting their homemade signs and waving foam Number One fingers, chanting the names of their favorite Kiss contestants. The press turned their cameras on the raucous crowd and began clicking.

"And . . . and . . . and THOSE FIVE . . ." Lorna tried, blinking rapidly.

"Miss Kiss ROCKS!"

"QUIEEEEEETTTT!" Lorna's cheeks shook ferociously as she bellowed into the microphone.

The crowd instantly quieted and foam fingers fell back into laps.

Lorna smirk-thanked them and smoothed down her skirt, as if she hadn't just yelled like a kindergarten teacher. "And those five will be put through our "Interpretive Dance" round. The lucky three who survive will be judged on beauty and their down-home Kissimmee style! And at the end of it all, we'll have our new MISSSS KISSSSSSSS!"

Everyone cheered again, and this time Lorna rolled with it, smiling like the applause was for her. "So without further ado, please meet our twenty young hopefuls!" She stepped off the stage, clapping as the red curtain lifted.

The string quartet busted out an instrumental version of Stevie Wonder's "Isn't She Lovely," and a line of girls wearing matching red gowns and Miss Kiss sashes appeared. Most of them were sweating already, but they still managed to project pure joy, as though they preferred it that way.

The song changed and the girls broke into a slightly off-key version of "What I Did for Love" from the hit Broadway musical *A Chorus Line*.

SAS were dead center. Sarah's wild blond hair had been tamed into a glamorous mini pony, showing off her high cheekbones and perfect nose. Sari had penciled in an upper lip—and from this distance it looked real. It was hard to spot Amandy at first, because she had cut long bangs that covered half her eyelids. At first Claire was shocked because there had been no mention of such a drastic move. But they brought attention to her deep blue eyes, making her even more EW than Claire could have imagined. She winked her approval and Amandy winked back her thanks. SAS had done well, and Claire felt proud to call them her FBFFs.

But it was Massie who really shocked Claire. She was standing at the very end of the line, looking more than pleased to be wearing the same red poly-blend dress as the other contestants. She hadn't added a single look-at-me adornment to her outfit, allowing her deep tan to do most of the heavy lifting. Her slightly wavy hair looked very natural, her makeup—several coats of Very Black mascara, a touch of gold eye shimmer and gloss—minimal. Next to a line of mostly blondes with sunburned shoulders and stiff updos, she looked relaxed, confident, and strangely passionate about show tunes.

We did what we had toooo doooooooooooooo.

Won't forget! Can't regret! What I did for love.

Claire took a long sip of complimentary lemonade while her friends worked their toothy pageant smiles in spite of the blazing heat. The cold, tart drink splashed against the back of her dry throat and reminded her once again how relieved she was to be behind the judges' table, not posed in front of it. Public evaluations, competing with friends, and faking confidence were part of life in Westchester. So why not enjoy this power position while she could? She smiled happily as the opening song ended and Lorna handed the microphone over to the mayor.

"Thank you, Lorna!" As Hammond kicked off the Speed Question-and-Answer round, every contestant looked at him with an expectant grin.

Except for four girls, who refused to take their eyes off Claire. And suddenly even the turbo fan and lemonade couldn't keep her from feeling the heat of the competition.

Mayor Reggie covered his burning scalp with the festive MISS KISS tank top from his gift bag. "Ahhhhhh," he smile-sighed into the microphone. "That's better."

The girls onstage giggled like they were watching a Will Ferrell movie. Claire figured that either the sight of the stately mayor with pink-ribbed cotton draped over his head looked ten times funnier from the stage, or the contestants were beyond nervous about the first round.

"Let me start by saying how lovely you ladies look this afternoon," Mayor Reggie began. The audience politely clapped their approval while the contestants squirm-beamed. "Now, the first round is what we like to call the Quick Kiss. The judges will take turns asking you surprise questions. You will do your best to respond quickly and intelligently. As Lorna said, the ten best will move on to our next round." He pulled the top index card off the pink stack in the center of the table and glanced at the first question. "Ready?"

The girls smiled and speed-nodded.

"The first question is for Gracie," the mayor said as he read the name at the top of the card.

The audience applauded as the perky redhead stepped forward.

"Gracie," he said with authority, "what do you expect to gain from this pageant?"

The girl grinned as if she had waited her entire life for this particular question.

"Life experience, friendships that will last an eternity and beyond, and the honor of representing our hometown!" She punched her fist in the air. The audience returned her enthusiasm with roof-raising applause.

Vonda took the next card in the stack. "Beth?"

A squat girl with a muscular gymnast's body, short black hair, and no makeup stepped forward. She was as far from stereotypical pageant type as Ugly Betty. In fact, rumor was she'd made the cut because there weren't enough dark-haired contestants this year and the association wanted some diversity.

Vonda cleared her throat. "Beth, what is the last cultural thing you did?"

"Easy. Ate at a taco stand with my cousin." A few people in the audience snickered. But Beth didn't mind. She stepped back into formation like a proud soldier.

Vonda passed the microphone. Claire, avoiding the desperate eyes of her friends, lifted a pink card off the stack.

OMG!

"May-sie," she said, purposely mispronouncing Massie's name to avoid any suspicion that the two were friends.

Massie stepped forward, chin high, shoulders back, jaw relaxed.

Had she really never done this before?

"Um, okay, at, uh, what point does a, um, girl become a woman?" Claire said to the card, too nervous to meet Massie's eyes. Her pits began to sweat. Was it obvious they knew each other? Would anyone figure out that they were currently sharing a bedroom? What if Massie choked? What if—

"A girl becomes a woman when she gets her own Visa," Massie blurted with a proud smile.

"What did she just say?" Vonda snapped, holding her hand over her heart in shock.

Claire gasped. A growing murmur swirled around her.

"A *travel* visa," Claire jumped in. "I like that. A girl who values the importance of traveling." Out of the corner of her eye, she saw Sari wince. Was she gassy? Faint? Peeved that Claire just helped—

Lorna quickly grabbed the microphone away from Claire and hissed, "Keep all comments to yourself, please."

"Sorry," Claire mouthed. She angled her body slightly closer to the fan. The cool blast of air instantly settled her.

"Next up is Amandy!" Reggie announced quickly, clearly trying to move things along. "Who do you think is the most popular person in the world?"

Come on, Amandy. . . . Say something good. . . .

Onstage, Amandy lowered her head and casually arranged her bangs over her eyes.

Claire clasped her hands together under the table. *Don't fuss. . . . Just answer the question. . . .*

As if she'd honed in on the telepathic plea, Amandy lifted her head. "God. God is the most popular person in the world."

Claire exhaled as the audience applauded. Lorna gave the judges a hurry-this-along wave.

Nodding at Lorna, Vonda picked up a card. "Caryn, what is the best quality parents can pass on to their children?"

"Food!" Caryn waved to her tan-times-ten mom, then stepped back.

"Thank you, Caryn." Vonda passed the mic to Claire while Caryn's mom clapped loudly from the third row.

Claire pursed her lips at the card, pretending she didn't notice Sari squirming again. "Nina, what's the biggest problem facing education today?"

A pair of jiggling D-cups stepped forward. "Homework on the weekends."

The audience roared approval while Nina, and her boobs, bounced back into line.

Reggie cleared his throat and mopped his beading forehead with the pink shirt. "Wendi, what do you want to do with your life?"

"Fight the war on terror. And win!" A bucktooth smile later, she took her place back in the Miss Kiss lineup.

"Sarah," Vonda said, tucking a lock of hair behind her ear.

Claire crossed her fingers and took a quick sip of lemonade.

"What is a recent goal you accomplished?"

Sarah proudly smoothed a hand over her scalp. "I managed to get my crazy hair into this sleek ponytail."

Everyone laughed—even Vonda.

"Deena," Claire read, making a point of *not* noticing Sari

fidgeting with the back of her dress. "Um, what is the biggest problem young people face today?"

Deena searched the crowd with her pea-green eyes, cocked her head to the side, and placed her hands on her narrow hips. "Stepmoms who think taking me to the mall one stupid afternoon will make up for the fact that *you stole my father*!"

A woman near the back gasped. Claire swiveled in her judge's chair just as several people stood to let a weeping redhead and a purple-faced man pass.

"Sari," Reggie quickly announced, tugging on a droopy earlobe. "Name the one thing about yourself you'd like to change."

Claire crossed her legs, then uncrossed them. She sat on her hands. Then she sent telepathic messages to her chat-happy friend: *Keep it short, Sari. . . . Keep it short, Sari. . . . Keep it short, Sari. . . .*

Sari stepped forward, her expression strained, like she was holding in a poo or about to have a baby or—

"Ahhhhhhhhhhhhhhhhhhhhhhhhhhhhhhhhhh!" She smacked her back and thrashed around like a trapped tuna. "Get it out!"

In an instant, Amandy reached down Sari's dress and smacked something lumpy to the ground. A spastic crab landed with a tap, then began snapping at her feet.

"Freak!" Sari kicked it, sending it straight for Jilly Lipper's left calf.

"Owwwwwww!" Jilly cry-pulled the crab off her bleeding leg and blindly whipped it over her shoulder . . . where it clamped on to Annie Laramie's cheek and hung like a fallen mountain climber, dangle-hanging for his life.

"Ehmagawsh!"

"Whose crab is that?!"

"I'm allergic to shellfish!"

"Is it . . . *possessed*?"

Suddenly, all of Toho Square erupted in crab-induced chaos. Claire was frozen in her chair in horror. Massie had retreated to a crab-free zone stage left, where she was laughing hysterically and taking pictures with her iPhone. Medics and parents were rushing the stage as the homicidal crab made its way from one screaming, flailing contestant to the next, pinching and plucking anyone who got in its way.

"Jaws!" Sari's father tore through the mayhem and pulled the crustacean off Lida Rosen's thigh. "Jaws, what are you doing here?" He hugged the crab, then his daughter, soothingly petting Jaws's pincers. The sight of Joe made Jaws relax—and Sari cry.

"What were you thinking?" Joe set Jaws on his shoulder and fixed Sari with a stern glare.

She weep-rubbed her clawed back, her upper lip hidden by a wave of salty tears. "Pinching makes me answer quickly," she hiccupped. "So I thought to myself, 'How can I get pinched during the pageant,' because that would have been super helpful. So then I thought about Jaws and decided to borrow him from the restaurant, thinking he would help me. . . ." She stopped and sobbed. "Oh, Daddy, I'll never make it to the Dance round." She buried herself in his white Hanes for Him T-shirt and bawled. Her father stroked her head with one hand and held Jaws at a safe distance with the other.

"Everyone please take your seats." Lorna tapped loudly on the microphone. "The crustacean has been captured. Our Kisses will be back as soon as the blood dries and the scores are tallied." She then marched over to Sari with a death-glare creased across her tan face. Claire's stomach dropped at the same time the red velvet curtain did, shielding the contestants from the snickering audience and clicking cameras.

More than anything, Claire wanted to race backstage and check in with her friends. But she was forced to hang with the judges and discuss why a girl would *ever* think pinching herself in a Speed Question-and-Answer round was a rational idea.

Gulp.

Twenty minutes later, Lorna retook the podium and addressed the wilting crowd. "The scores have been tabulated. The finalists chosen. And here are the five girls who were not injured *and* who scored a minimum of twenty-five out of thirty points in the first round!"

"Go Gracie!"

"Jillyyyyyy!"

"Kiss me, Caryn!"

The red velvet curtain lifted. Gracie, Sarah, Wendi, Amandy, Massie (and *Bean!*) stood in a semicircle, each wearing the costume suited to their world issue of choice.

They smiled graciously as the audience applauded their staying power.

Claire's heart sank when she thought of Sari, who was probably backstage covered in Neosporin and claw marks, mourning her short-lived career on the beauty pageant circuit. But she took comfort in knowing that the eights she'd given SAM had advanced them to the next round. Her fairness plan was working beautifully.

When the clapping ceased, Lorna smiled, revealing a smear of Paradise Pink lipstick across her left eyetooth. "Gracie, please step up and share your issue with us."

The graceful redhead, who was dressed in a nude-colored unitard, stepped forward. "My issue is obesity in America." She lowered her head and waited for the music to cue.

Suddenly, the sound of crunching potato chips crackled from the speakers. Then came the slurping of soda. Soon, the slobbering, lip-smacking, finger-licking noises of someone gorging herself on greasy food fused into a rhythmic beat. Gracie pushed out her belly and puffed up her cheeks and proceeded to jazz-walk to stage left. During a particularly loud slurp, she stopped midstride in an exaggerated attempt to catch her breath.

Claire peered out at the audience—many of whom were clear junk-food eaters themselves—but most people were leaning forward and nodding thoughtfully, as if they, too, hated fast food with a fiery vengeance.

Onstage, Gracie busted out an energetic hip-hop sequence. After an ill-fated pop-lock, she stopped and held two fingers to her wrist to check her pulse. The eating sounds got louder and her bursts of energy got shorter, until finally she collapsed on the ground in a distended heap.

After three bows, several curtsies, and scattered applause, Gracie cleared the way for Sarah.

"My issue is the earthquake that scientists predict will hit California in the next thirty years." She lifted two fistfuls of mud and smeared them all over her white Danskin tracksuit.

Well, shake it up baby now . . .

From the moment the Beatles' "Twist and Shout" started playing, Sarah began thrashing. There was no slow build, like Claire had encouraged. No moment of tranquility *before* the disaster struck. She simply flailed from one side of the stage to the other like she had been pumped full of Red Bull and tossed into the nearest mosh pit to work off the excess energy.

Claire stress-bit her lower lip. How was she ever going to convince Mayor Reggie and Vonda that this performance was EW?

After several spastic rotations around the stage, Sarah fell to the ground and began convulsing.

The crowd gasped collectively and Claire struggled to contain the nerve-tremors in her stomach.

A familiar, concerned woman's voice rose above the music. "I think she's hurt!" Sarah's mother stood up in the second row. "Medic!"

Seconds later, the same team that had rushed the stage to rescue the girls from Jaws arrived to rescue Sarah from herself.

"What are you doing?" she shouted just before they restrained her and stuck a stick in her mouth. "Uhm ine!" she tried, but they didn't believe she was *fine* and hauled her off, kicking and screaming.

Lorna signaled to the soundman to cut the sound track, and "Twist and Shout" ended midlyric.

Claire shot Amandy a look of concern. But Amandy's relieved smile suggested that she was anything but distraught over her competitor-slash-BFF's sudden elimination.

Meanwhile, Mayor Reggie nodded at Wendi, urging her to take the stage and fill the awkward moment.

"My issue is terrorism." Wendi stepped forward, dressed in a camouflage miniskirt, matching racerback tank, and three-inch platforms. Her long limbs had been slicked in bronzing oil, her eye makeup was smoky, and her hair had been teased to Pamela Anderson proportions.

"Does she want to fight terrorists or seduce them?" Vonda mumbled.

Claire and Reggie snickered.

With no music, just several grunts and hai-ahs, Wendi busted out a series of karate kicks that would only prove one thing to the enemy: that Wendi preferred thong underwear to full coverage.

Claire heard Todd whoop extra loudly before Judi covered his eyes and shushed him.

Amandy and her flattering new bangs were next. She managed to touch the crowd with her beautifully portrayed account of global warming. It was an EW performance—maybe even nineworthy.

Massie was the last to take center stage. Dressed in a formfitting white shift dress that had been patched together using several different PETA T-shirts, she stepped forward with grace and confidence. With the snap of a finger, Bean raced out from the wings and leapt into her arms. "My issue is makeup testing on animals," Massie announced. Bean barked once.

"Awwwwwwww!" The crowd aw-clapped their approval.

While Claire was just as charmed as the rest of the audience, a part of her was terrified, like she was careening down a hill on a bike with no brakes. The moment of choosing between her friends was rapidly approaching. Massie *had* to at least be on par with Amandy.

Massie snapped her fingers again, and Pink's old hit, "Get the Party Started," blared out of the loudspeakers.

Get this party started on a Saturday night
Everybody's waiting for me to arrive

Massie "borrowed" a few modern dance moves from Alicia's jazz routine (Gawd knew Alicia had performed it a billion times for the PC), pulling them off flawlessly while Bean scampered at her feet. After a minute, she stopped in front of an imaginary mirror and mimed putting on makeup.

As Massie applied invisible eye shadow, Bean suddenly froze and yelped in pain. When she brushed on blush, Bean collapsed. And with a final swipe of mascara, Bean rolled over and played dead.

"No!" the audience gasped.

A seven-year-old girl in a princess costume started sniffling, but Massie, still in character, acted totally oblivious to the animal carcass. She danced away from the crime scene like a giddy girl anxious to meet her friends for a night on the town.

The music stopped, and Bean lay on center stage, her legs stiff, poking straight up to the heavens. After a beat everyone applauded. A few wiped their eyes. Then they stood, giving the PETA performance the ovation it deserved.

Claire stood too, her teeth chattering with pride.

After the judges' scores from the issues segment had been tallied and the audience quieted once more, Lorna leaned into the microphone. "And now it's time for Beauty, our third and final round. Our judges will be looking for the girls who best represent innocence, poise, and polish. Behold, the three remaining Kisses . . ."

As the curtain lifted, the audience let out an appreciative sigh. No one seemed surprised to see Amandy, Gracie, and Massie smiling graciously in their eveningwear—except for Claire, who nearly spit out her lemonade. For some reason, Amandy was wearing the tight black Geren Ford cocktail dress Massie had fallen in love with at Saks . . . and Massie was dressed in the dusty rose Theory three-tier gown Claire had picked out for her.

What was going on? Claire's insides felt like a battlefield of emotions, each one fighting to be heard. Part of her was honored times ten that Massie had taken her advice. But the other part was horrified that Amandy had been manipulated into wearing an outfit that had Vonda and Reggie shifting uncomfortably in their seats. In Kissimmee, there was nothing EW about that dress.

Claire wiped her sweaty palms on her skirt. The best she

could do was hope that Gracie would get tangled up in her Easter egg yellow tulle gown and crash into the string quartet. But no such luck. She walked the stage with giraffelike grace, her red curls bobbing like the steady beating heart of a pageant winner who knew she had a lifetime of sashes and tiaras ahead of her.

Stress seemed to add five degrees to the temperature. Claire hooked a Ked around the neck of the floor fan and scooted it closer, all the while taking soothing fire-breaths.

Amandy followed Gracie across the stage, walking to the beat of disapproving whispers. Her dark hair, long bangs, and black dress made her look like the kind of girl who kicked Miss Kiss winners around for cardio.

Claire toe-dragged the fan even closer, but suddenly it caught on the stage floor. The rotating head got knocked off its locked position and started shooting air directly at the stage . . . directly at Amandy. As she stopped on the edge for the required three seconds, a giant gust blew right into her face. In an instant, her bangs were lifted off her forehead, revealing giant scabs where her eyebrows used to be.

Gasp!

Amandy's hands flew to her forehead.

"Alien!"

"Mommy, what's wrong with her?!"

"Ehmagawsh!" Claire quickly leaned over and repositioned the fan. But it was too late. Several children screamed. Vonda choked on her lemonade, and Mayor Reggie turned away in horror.

"Thanks a lot!" Amandy shouted at Claire before speed-finishing her beauty walk. Claire's intestines oscillated like the fan. Even though the disaster had been an accident, guilt had grabbed hold of her neck and started wringing.

While Massie dazzled the crowd with her relaxed confidence and pretty pink dress, Amandy tried to wipe away the black mascara that was dripping down her cheeks. The whole thing was totally EW.

And not in a good way.

The audience milled around restlessly while the press interviewed the rejects. The only people still sitting were the three judges.

Lorna stood above their table, waving her red Lucite clipboard in front of her face to cool her slick forehead. "That was quite a round," she whisper-snickered to the judges, then instantly regained her composure. "Now, if each of you would please write the name of the girl you feel best represents this year's Miss Kiss, and drop it in here"—she shook an empty shoe box that had been covered in silver aluminum foil—"we can all get home to our air conditioners."

"No more numbers?" Claire muttered.

"Nope. This is do or die," Reggie explained, wringing out his head-tee.

Claire tapped a Sharpie against her front teeth and stared at the red velvet curtain. She'd only planned for EW. She had no strategy for "do or die."

Massie was clearly better than Amandy. So was Gracie. But this had been Amandy's dream since the day they met. Yet, if she voted for Amandy, Lorna would get suspicious. Between the dress, the scabs, and the sobs, it was impossible to justify her over the other two. . . . *Ugh!* How was she supposed to be *fair* about this?

With certainty, Mayor Reggie and Vonda dropped their crumpled pieces of paper in the silver shoe box. Then they slid it down the table to Claire.

"Tough call," Claire tried. But they both looked at her like that was the furthest thing from the truth.

So in the heat of the moment, and in the name of fairness, Claire finally made her pick for Miss Kiss. She shut her eyes, gulped back some courage, then wrote GRACIE in thick black Sharpie letters and jammed it in the box.

Suddenly Claire's phone vibrated.

Amandy: No you did nawt!

Claire whip-turned around and saw SAS hovering behind her, identical angry expressions on their sweaty faces. Her palms started to sweat. More than anything she wanted to explain how hard she had tried to help them. How badly she wanted them to win. How much she hated having to choose. But she was trapped at the judges' table, under the scrutiny of Vonda, Reggie, and Lorna, forced to act like an impartial robot while her three FBFFs linked arms and Red Rovered off in anger.

"Thank you, judges. I will see you at the crowning!" Lorna smiled like she wasn't crabby and damp and marched across the stage.

As Reggie and Vonda stood and said goodbye, a dry lump formed in the back of Claire's throat that the lemonade couldn't quench. With trembling hands and shortness of breath, Claire began texting.

I tried to help you all equally, I swear . . . Eights all the way . . . Our lucky number! Voting for Gracie was the only fair thing I could do.

While she waited anxiously for a response, Claire searched the crowd for Massie, wondering if SAS had told her the news, praying they hadn't. Claire's eyes finally locked on Massie, who was greeting her admirers. But if they had told her, the alpha seemed far from concerned as she and Bean posed for pictures for the press and a cluster of fans.

Claire jumped when her phone vibrated loudly on the table.

Amandy: Was it fair the way U "helped" Sari by telling her to pinch herself? Or told Sarah 2 dance like
an earthquake? Or me 2 get my brows ripped out with
burning hot wax? Admit it. U wanted us to lose so UR
BFF Massie could win.
Claire: I was trying to help!!!!!!

Claire wiped the tears from her eyes, wishing SAS could see her. Maybe then they'd know how wrong they were.

But it was too late.

Amandy was in the distance, showing Lorna the text message she had just received.

Instantly, Lorna fixed her eyes on Claire. She stuck out her neck, bent slightly, and, like a raging bull, charged straight for her.

"Is this true?" She waved Amandy's cell in front of Claire's wet blue eyes.

The press began to gather. Then other Kisses. And then Massie.

"Did you *fix* the contest?" Her cheeks were flushed and her *J*-bob had flattened to an *I*.

"Um, no?" Claire tried.

"Then explain *this*." Lorna began reading the text while the press scribbled her words on the backs of their programs.

The crowd gasped, and Bean yipped loudly when Lorna read the part about Massie.

"Your judge days are *over*, Miss Lyons." Lorna tore up Claire's stipend check for the cameras. "Just like your film career."

"But—" Claire tried, but a big saliva bubble came out of her mouth where all the right words should have been.

Mayor Reggie, Vonda, and the rest of the crowd glared at Claire as if she'd just peed in the public pool. Tears began trickling down her face. Not only for the lost friends or the lost check. But for the lost hope. This was the last time she'd ever do anything for anyone again.

The only person who seemed to appreciate her was Gracie, who failed to realize that removing Claire's vote made it a tie. And a tie meant the audience at the Miss Kiss Coronation Ball tomorrow night would decide the winner. No, Gracie didn't quite get that yet. Because she thank-hugged Claire so hard, the coarse tulle from her yellow dress scratched a big red mark right in the middle of her forehead, shaped like an *L*.

No one said a word on the car ride home. Not even Todd.
There were no lectures on fairness and honesty. No inquiries
as to what Claire could have possibly been thinking. No
suggestions on how she could mend her broken friendships.
Everyone just focused on the Carrie Underwood CD Judi had
gotten last Mother's Day and let Claire cry in peace.

When they got home, Massie's limo was in the driveway. Jay mumbled something to his wife, then parked on the
street.

Knowing Massie was home filled Claire with the same kind
of anxiety she got when someone told her they had a surprise
for her. Like something dangerous might be lurking . . .

"Dinner's in an hour," Judi announced when they entered
the air-conditioned house. Everyone nodded, then went their
separate ways.

Claire stood alone in the foyer and sighed. Was it her imag-
ination or did the white wicker hallway furniture seem disap-
pointed in her too?

Wearily and with grave heaviness, she climbed the peach-
carpeted stairs as if underwater, desperate to collapse on
the AeroBed and document her sadness with a series of self-
portraits she'd call "Kiss This!"

When she reached the second floor, the sight of her bedroom door made her tear up all over again. Covered in old Hello Kitty stickers, it reminded her of happier times. Easier times. Times filled with innocent laughter shared by four best friends with one brain.

Bracing herself, Claire pressed her ear against Tropical Island Kitty but heard nothing. Maybe Massie wasn't home. Or maybe she was lying in bed watching *Gossip Girl* on her iPod, waiting to laugh about the whole thing. After all, she hadn't even heard of Miss Kiss until a week ago.

Claire reached for her doorknob. It was now or—

LOCKED!

"Massie?" she jiggled the knob.

"Go away!" Massie called.

In an instant, Claire's sadness switched to anger like she was changing tracks on a playlist. "This is *my* room!"

"You take from me, I take from you."

"What did I take from you?" Claire yelled at Scuba Kitty.

"I was the best," Massie insisted through the door. "I should have won."

Claire kicked Disco Kitty with her Ked. "Let me in and I'll explain!"

"Explain what?" Massie asked, opening the door a crack. Claire's room was covered in clothes. "Why you betrayed me?"

The alpha was wearing a black satin robe, her face covered in a green mud mask. All she needed was a broomstick and—

"Gawd, I have *nuh-thing* to wear to the ball tomorrow!"

She kicked a red Valentino dress that accidentally landed on Bean's bed. The dog woke with a start, looked around, then curled up and lowered her head in chiffon.

"What do you mean? There are clothes everywhere," Claire pointed out, happy to change the subject. She could hear her mom shuffling around in the kitchen downstairs.

"These are for *winners*, Kuh-laire." Massie picked up a purple Marni blouse and tossed it over her head. "Ugh!"

"But you *are* a winner," Claire said, stepping over a sea foam green Marc Jacobs tote to enter her room.

Massie stopped and looked at Claire, her amber eyes smoldering. "What if I lose that audience vote? Then I'll be a number two. And I have no idea how to dress like a number two." She folded her arms across her chest and opened her mouth, which was starting to tighten from the mask. "Any advice?"

"Massie, I'm sorry." Claire looked at the white shag, willing the burning feeling behind her eyeballs to go away.

"For what? Voting for a yellow-wearing stranger? Or telling me you were working all week while you were helping your *real* friends."

Claire's stomach flipped. "How do you know about that?"

Massie grabbed a fistful of hundred-dollar bills off her night table. "Benjamin here managed to get it out of your brother."

Claire felt like she was falling off a cliff and everyone she knew was leaning over the edge, happily waving goodbye. "I was trying to—"

"Well, whatever you were *trying* to do didn't work," Massie spat through her tightening lips. "Unless your goal was to make Gracie win."

Something inside Claire snapped.

"Why are you so upset?" she heard herself shout. "You don't even live here. You didn't grow up dreaming about this contest. You didn't even know what it was until you randomly showed up."

Massie opened her mouth. Tiny fissures cracked the surface of her mask. "I'm upset, Kuh-laire, because I flewhereaftermy parentsblewmeoffforsomelameEuro-cruiseandwhenIgothere mythingswerebeingransackedbyabunchofdirtylocalsandthen youditch-liedtomeallweeksoyoucouldhangwiththemandthen youvotedforGracie!"

For a minute, Claire stopped breathing.

She forgot all about SAS and the pageant and Gracie and the number eight. Massie had never shared her feelings like that before. Even though she'd referred to Claire's friends as dirty locals, her confession was rarer than steak tartare and touching times ten.

Claire placed a sympathetic hand on Massie's robed shoulder. She couldn't imagine being left to fend for herself while her parents took a joyride around the Mediterranean. "Did your parents really blow you off?"

Massie wiggled out from under her grip. "Relax, Dr. Phil. They bought me a ticket. I didn't want to go."

"Oh." Claire's compassion snapped back like a retractable tape measure. "I was just trying to be a good friend."

"Like you even know what that means," Massie mumbled, tightening her belt around her waist.

Claire's eyes welled up with tears. She wanted to race for the comfort of her bed, but it had been taken over by Massie and Bean. So she paced, mindfully avoiding the designer land mines that dotted her floor like a war zone.

"Just so you know, the only reason I agreed to be a judge in the first place was so I could get the check and buy the clothes on your stupid back-to-school shopping list! But for what? So I could trade in my Keds for Kors? Gawd, I don't even know if I like Mitchell Kors."

"Michael," Massie mumbled through the hardened mask.

Claire stepped over a Louboutin flat. "I have no idea *what* I like anymore. Who I like. What I wear. Who I am!" She pulled her blond hair in frustration.

"Add a *B* and an *R* to that *L* on your forehead and you'll know who you are." Massie sat down next to Bean and stroked her silky ears.

Claire smirked. "I already told you: I was just trying to be a good friend." Her voice was a little calmer now.

"To who?" Massie asked like a ventriloquist, her mouth barely moving. "Those girls? Gawd, Kuh-laire, they don't deserve you. If they were such good friends, they wouldn't be blaming you for their own mistakes."

"You're right." Claire smiled brightly, like the warm sun after a violent storm. "Thanks." She paused. "So you forgive me?"

"Puh-lease!" Massie's mask cracked. Green mud chips fell to the carpet. "You are so out of the Pretty Committee."

"What? *Why?*" Claire swallowed hard, pushing her beating heart back down into her chest. *Out* of the PC? She felt a quake of nausea and grabbed the door frame for support. Why didn't anyone understand she'd just been trying to help? "You just said they were lame for blaming me. And now you're—"

Massie crossed her legs and narrowed her eyes under her mask. "Unlike your FLBRs, I'm not blaming you because I sucked and I can't admit it. I'm blaming you because I was the best and you didn't pick me." She glared at Claire with the confidence of someone whose face wasn't flaking all over her robe. "I just want what I deserve."

"Well, so do I." Claire held her ground.

"You already got what you deserved, Kuh-laire!" Massie grabbed her Chanel face wash and slammed the door behind her, leaving Claire all alone to deal with the mess.

Claire gazed up at the dark clouds over Toho Square and pray-begged for a hurricane. The forecast called for showers, but not until midnight. Which wouldn't help at all. She needed a way out, *now*.

Her parents weren't buying the whole stomach-bug excuse; rather, they'd stopped buying it once Claire mowed down an entire container of KFC macaroni salad for lunch. She'd claimed a migraine around four o'clock, and then had gotten busted blasting Ashlee Simpson's "Rule Breaker" in her bedroom. At six, she'd broken down and admitted the real reason she didn't want to go to the Miss Kiss crowning: Everyone hated her. But that didn't work either. Her father grabbed Claire by the shoulders, gave her a slight shake, and then asked:

"What's your last name?"

"Lyons," Claire mumbled.

"And what do Lyons do?"

"Roar."

"I can't hear you," Jay bellowed.

"RRRROAR!" Claire managed.

"Good." Jay released his grip, satisfied. "I know it's been tough for you the last few weeks. And I know you made some decisions you regret. So show up at the ball tonight, apologize to the people you hurt, and move on, Claire-Bear."

The childish nickname made her tear up.

"If you act like it's over, they'll act like it's over. And before you know it everyone will move on to the next scandal." He stated it like it was no big deal to be publicly shamed in the town square, then disowned by your friends. "Now go get dressed—we don't want to be late. Massie spent all day at the spa getting ready and we want to be there on time to support her."

Claire zipped up last summer's multicolored striped J.Crew dress, wondering why Massie needed *support* after spa-ing all day. Wasn't it Claire who'd risked her reputation to help her friends, and then gotten dumped, fired, and scorned? Where was *her* support?

But, as always, she took her father's advice and feigned pride while she waited at the gates of Toho Square to cast her audience vote for Miss Kiss. And this time there was no question whose name she'd write on the ballot.

The scene was magical: Red China balls hung from the sleepy branches of the square's weeping willows. A festive gold tent covered the chairs that faced the stage. Anticipation—or was it the random whips of lightning?—made the humid, almost metallic-scented air feel electrically charged. Dogs barked in the distance. Bursts of children's laughter added punch to the steady hum of mingle-chatter. And violin music tied it all together into one charming little package. . . .

Or at least, it *would* have been charming if all the guests hadn't been whisper-pointing at Claire as she inched her way inside.

While her brother offered free T-Odd Jobs calendars to anyone with hands and her parents greeted their friends, Claire channeled her inner Britney. She was bouncing back from her scandals, wasn't she? Claire held her chin high, trying to act like she had just as much right to be there as anyone else.

When she reached the voting table, she nodded hello to Lorna, and held her ballot over the box to—

"What do you think you're doing?" A plump, French-manicured hand swatted Claire's wrist away.

"Voting," Claire managed despite her sudden case of dry mouth.

"Not here, you're not." Lorna plucked the paper from Claire's hand, read it, and then tossed it in the trash.

A young mother-daughter team snickered into their palms while an eight-year-old boy loser-sneezed nearby.

"Ms. Crowley Brown." Jay stepped forward. "With all due respect—"

"It's fine, Dad." Claire tugged her father's arm. "Let's just go inside, okay?"

"But—"

"Dad, *please*."

He met his daughter's pleading eyes and, for the first time ever, decided to forgo the pep lecture.

"Very well." Jay dropped his ballot in the box, waited for Judi and Todd to do the same, then brushed past Lorna with a haughty *tsk*.

Once Claire placed one Kedded foot inside, a man shouted, "Look, it's the Lying Lyon!" He pushed back the brim on his black GREETINGS, ORLANDO! cap and lifted his camera.

Before Claire had a chance to react, photographers surrounded her and started clicking. Claire's vision instantly became obstructed—not by flashes or infamy-panic, but by a mass of shaggy red hair.

Todd had thrown himself in front of his sister, shielding her from the paparazzi's scandal-hungry lenses, while proudly displaying his new calendar. Sure, it wasn't the most selfless move in the world, but it, along with the proud way her parents were flanking her, made Claire realize she wasn't completely alone. This made her feel that she could hold her head high, despite the unforgiving glares and whispers . . . until SAS grazed by like complete strangers, sending Claire's short-lived confidence to its grave.

"Are you *okay* with that?" Judi asked, sounding slightly snubbed herself.

"Of course not, Mom," Claire whisper-hissed, hoping no one could overhear the pathetic details of her social life. She pulled Judi away from the crowd and into a corner. "But what am I supposed to do?"

"Have you tried apologizing?"

"For what? Trying to help?" Claire snapped, immediately regretting her sarcasm. "Sorry."

Judi grinned her forgiveness. "They're upset they didn't win. And it's easier to blame you than themselves. Give it time."

The word *time* echoed in Claire's mind, bolstering her from a place of sadness to one of thoughtfulness, which was soon followed by rage. SACS had one week left together before she moved back north, and this was how they wanted to spend it? In a fight? Over a pageant? A pageant that was notorious for breaking up (F)BFFs? They had to know deep down inside that Claire had been trying to help them. Trying to be a good friend. Trying to be fair. And if they didn't, they were about to.

"Be right back," she told her parents, who were starting to settle into their seats with the rest of the crowd.

"Roaaaar!" Jay growled.

Claire hurried away, distancing herself from the embarrassing family motto.

But a sudden drumroll sent her right back to her chair.

Once everyone was seated, the Kissimmee Chamber Orchestra began an instrumental version of Christina Aguilera's "Beautiful." At first, a few heads turned, then a few more. And before long everyone was ooooh-ing and ahhh-ing as the two finalists entered through the back of the tent and began walking down the pink petal-covered aisle, side by side, toward the stage.

Massie, dressed in a gold silk chiffon dress with black roses across the bust, was breathtaking. Her tan had been dusted in bronze shimmer, and her glossy hair was in a purposely messy updo. Her purple hair streak was made to look like it accidentally fell from the diamond "lips" that clipped it all together. But Claire knew better. Bean pranced by her black rose–covered slides, wearing a gold blazer and matching pillbox hat.

The audience reached into the aisles desperate to touch her, congratulate her—or, for the lucky ones—snap a quick picture. She smiled graciously in the face of fandemonium, slowing to be admired but never stopping.

Gracie, despite her perfect posture, toothy grin, and frilly floral gown, was almost invisible next to Massie Block.

The winner was clear. And once the girls took their spots on the special-edition red Hershey's Kiss–covered stage, Lorna made it official. Massie covered her mouth in faux modesty and lift-hugged Bean while Gracie blinked back her tears and embraced the alpha.

"Massie! Massie! Massie! Massie!" The crowd cheered and chanted and stomped their feet. Silver balloons dropped from above and the audience stood.

Claire got up with the rest of them but couldn't bring herself to applaud. Her fists were clenched, her lips curved in a frown. How *dare* Massie crash *her* party? How *dare* she take this honor away from a Florida native who truly wanted it just to satisfy her ego? How *dare* she act like Claire's Gracie vote might have cost her the tiara?

"And now, the moment everyone's been waiting for!" Lorna hopped up and down on her cankles as Vonda brought out a large red bundle.

Massie's pleased expression shifted faster than the storm clouds when Lorna held up the official Miss Kiss dress. The stiff red gown was covered in sequins, from the floor-sweeping hem straight up to the puffy sleeves. It was shaped like a triangle but made for a square.

Claire brushed her bangs out of her eyes. Was this really the same dress she had coveted all those years?

"Massie, I am pleased to present you with the official Miss Kiss dress!" Lorna thrust it toward her. But the alpha waved it away like used toilet paper.

Lorna's grin faltered. In an obvious attempt to avoid a scene, she pulled Massie aside and smiled through their conversation, just in case people were watching. A minute later they called Gracie over.

"Um, excuse me, everyone." Lorna ech-hemmed into the microphone. "I just received word that our crowned Miss Kiss has been accepted to a prestigious private school in Westchester and will not be able to perform the required Miss Kiss duties."

And just like that, a new Miss Kiss was anointed, and *she* couldn't *wait* to wear the dress.

Everyone formed the traditional line in front of Gracie to congratulate her and wish her well. And that's when Claire spotted SAS.

They had pushed their way toward the front, clamoring to be seen with the winner while the cameras were still interested.

"Be right back." Claire hurried off before her father could roar again.

"Hey," she said sadly, tapping SAS on the shoulders.

They harrumphed and turned away.

"Hey," Claire tried again. But they didn't even look at her. Instead they dug their hands into a shared bag of chocolate-covered pretzels while inching closer to Gracie.

One . . . two . . . three . . . inhale . . . and . . .

"You guys, I'm sorry, okay! Sorry you didn't win. But you have to believe that I wanted you to." Still no one said a word. The frustration that came with being misunderstood and ignored jacked up Claire's heart rate and made her insides tremble: An emotional geyser was about to erupt.

With tears flooding her eyes, Claire stomped her foot and turned to face her so-called FBFFs. "I *cheated* for you. Lost my check—for you! And have been nicknamed the Lying Lion by the press—because of you."

Still nothing.

Claire sniffled. "I have one week left here. Do you really want to spend it like this?"

Amandy lifted her blue eyes to meet Claire's. "No, we don't."

Claire's shoulders dropped. She exhaled. She felt instantly lighter. "Good."

"But it's either us or *her*."

Claire gasped like someone who had just been slapped in the face. The decision shouldn't have been too difficult considering Massie had kicked her out of the Pretty Committee. But still. She resented being asked to make it.

"Why do I have to *choose*? Why can't I be friends with all of you? Equally?"

Onstage, Gracie took another bow and adjusted her glimmering tiara.

"Because we're not all *equal*!" Amandy huffed. "When are you going to realize that?"

"We've known you longer!" Sarah insisted.

"Much longer," Sari added. "Like six years longer. Maybe even more. Or is it four years? Wait, maybe it's nine. . . ."

While SAS bicker-tried to figure it out, Claire fired off a quick text to Massie.

I know UR not tking 2 me but if you were would U make me choose between U and them?

Massie responded immediately.

Massie: No. I know U'd choose me.
Claire: How do U know?
Massie: What would U rather?

Claire flashed back to her first horrific sleepover at Massie's house. The girls had asked her if she'd rather be a) a friendless loser or b) have a ton of friends who secretly hated her. Back then her answer had been b. But now that she knew what it was like to have friends who secretly hated her, Claire's answer had changed.

"You know what, SAS?"

Three sets of eyes turned and looked her.

"I've made my choice." Claire turned on the heels of her brown and blue polka-dot Keds and waved goodbye.

"You're choosing *her*?" Amandy gasped.

"Nope," Claire yelled over her shoulder.

"Then who are you choosing?" Sara called after her.

"Me!" Claire shouted, not looking back.

The rain was starting to fall in thick, heavy drops, like they had been building up for a while. Everyone scattered for the parking lot.

Claire knew her decision was the right one. Even Todd seemed to think so. But still, her walk to the car seemed like an endless journey filled with deep sighs and nail-biting self-doubt. Miss Kiss was done. SACS was done. Orlando was—

"Well, look who it is," Jay called out to the girl sitting on the hood of his red Pontiac Torrent holding her dog.

Claire lifted her eyes.

"Hey," Massie said sweetly, twirling her purple streak. Her gold dress was spotted with raindrops, but she didn't seem to mind.

The Lyonses instinctively stopped walking. Claire instinctively kept going.

"Where's your limo?"

"I let him go." Massie looked out at the snaking line of cars waiting to get out of the lot.

Claire nodded, too weak to figure out what to say next.

Massie popped open her black rose–covered clutch. "Here." She reached inside and pulled out a pink slip of paper. "This is for you."

Claire kept her eyes on the alpha while she took it. Then she looked down.

"Huh?" she said to the one-thousand-dollar check in her hand.

"It's my first-place prize." Massie beamed.

Claire handed it back. "Congratulations."

Massie pushed Claire's hand away. "It's for you."

"Why?" Claire was too confused to feel anything but tired.

"Take it. You earned it." Massie gave Bean a gentle kiss on her forehead. "You worked just as hard on this pageant as anyone."

Claire looked away. The rain seemed to have gotten heavier. Puddles began forming by the Pontiac's tires, and people started running for their cars.

"I don't need charity," Claire stated. The rain was making her bangs split into a soggy blond *M*.

"It's nawt *charity*, Kuh-laire." Massie leaned over Bean to keep her dry. "I did it for me."

"Why? Because you feel guilty?" Claire pushed her wet bangs aside. "Because you understand why I did what I did? Because you miss me? Because you want me back in the Pretty Committee?"

Massie half smiled. And like a ray of sunshine, it made Claire's cool wet skin suddenly feel a little warmer. "Because I want you to buy some clothes."

"Why?" Claire's teeth began to chatter.

"Because I don't want my best friend dressing like an LBR in the eighth grade."

Claire giggled. And then they hugged.

In one more week, they'd be home.

Make sure you're **IN** on all the summer secrets.

STATE OF THE UNION

IN	OUT
✓ Purple hair streaks	Summer secrets
✓ Confidentiality contracts	
✓ Euro pop stars	
✓ Shark-tooth necklaces	
✓ Massie & Claire in Orlando	

Five girls. Five stories. One ah-mazing summer.

THE CLIQUE
SUMMER COLLECTION
BY LISI HARRISON

Summer may be over,
but eighth grade's just getting started.

P.S. I LOATHE YOU
Coming February 2009.

COMING TO DVD IN FALL 2008

THE CLIQUE
MOVIE

ALWAYS KNOW THE CURRENT STATE OF THE UNION

REGISTER FOR UPDATES AT

THECLIQUEMOVIE.COM

Five Ah-Mazing Stories.
One Ah-Dorable Must-Have
CLIQUE Gift Set!

The CLIQUE Ah-Mazing Collector's Gift Set Includes:

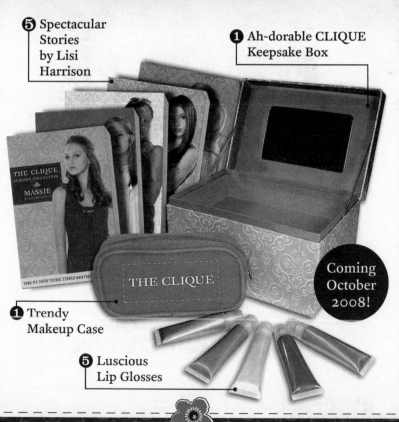

5 Spectacular Stories by Lisi Harrison

1 Ah-dorable CLIQUE Keepsake Box

1 Trendy Makeup Case

5 Luscious Lip Glosses

Coming October 2008!

Welcome to Poppy.

A poppy is a beautiful blooming red flower
(like the one on the spine of this book). It is also
the name of the new home of your favorite series.

Poppy takes the real world and makes it
a little funnier, a little more fabulous.

Poppy novels are wild, witty, and inspiring.
They were written just for you.

So sit back, get comfy, and pick a Poppy.

poppy

www.pickapoppy.com